Ponce

What *Actually* Happened at the Fountain of Youth

ALSO BY JIM HALVERSON

*Trials and Trails: Adventures and
Unexpected Discoveries of Life*

*Wilderness Spa: Where Physical Survival
Meets Psychological Survival*

What *Actually* Happened at the Fountain of Youth

JIM HALVERSON

Gail Force Publishing

Tallahassee Times

MAJOR FIND:

The chronicles of Ponce de Leon's second expedition to Florida have been found.

Scholars have documented Ponce de Leon's life from his youth in the court of Ferdinand and Isabella to his first expedition to Florida, but until now we have had precious little information about his second expedition to the western north shores of Florida, his quest for the Fountain of Youth, and the injuries he received.

Two Florida State geology students found the pages written by Ponce de Leon's chronicler in a dry limestone cave in the northwest panhandle. The original Spanish papers, five hundred years old, were found in relatively good shape, protected from time and moisture in a heavy triple-walled leather case.

The students turned the case and sensitive papers over to the university museum. The university called upon the Smithsonian documentation preservation team to protect them. The papers are safe and have been reproduced for public viewing. ∎

Editor's Notes:

- The parchment has been dated to the sixteenth century.
- Most of the ink has been dated to sixteenth-century Spain.
- Interestingly, the final pages were written with an ink totally different than the ink used in most of the manuscript. Chemical analysis revealed that the ink contained dyes available only from materials found in Northern Florida.

*The following account
completes the story of Ponce de Leon.*

PONCE

Juan fastened the final buttons on Isabella's embroidered silk gown. Isabella turned to face him and asked, "Are you sure you want to go fight the Moors in Granada? It's so far away, and they fight with long, sharp swords."

"If the king catches us, he'll cut parts off both of us with a dull, rusty sword. Some parts I'd like to keep for a while."

"He wouldn't do anything to me. He'd lose over half our empire. Besides, he's not worrying about us. He's totally consumed with containing the Portuguese navy."

"Well, good for you. I'm happy about that. I wish I had an empire for my security."

"Maybe someday. Do you want to go to church?"

"I don't want to confess this; I'll take my chances with silence."

"No, no, silly. We won't do that today. I want to get you blessed before you go into battle."

"Well, okay then."

Isabella led Juan from her bedroom suite and down the secured corridor to the Hall of Portraits. Halfway down the hall, they had stopped to admire a portrait recently hung, when Ferdinand called out, "Juan, what are you doing here?"

Juan's knees nearly buckled, cold sweat ran down his spine, and visions of rusty-sword decapitation flashed through his head. He was about to soil his pantaloons. The beautiful and sturdy building in which he stood, the Alcazar de Segovia, built on a high rock outcropping, protected the royal family and friends. Now Juan thought it more an inescapable prison.

The king continued, "You're going to miss your Latin lessons."

Juan swallowed hard and managed to speak in a weak voice. "Majesty, the queen asked me to accompany her to the church."

"Juan is going to Granada to fight the good fight. I'm going to get him blessed at San Miguel de Segovia."

"Oh, Juan Ponce de Leon, I am so proud of you." Ferdinand walked quickly toward Juan, reached into his pocket and pressed a small medal into Juan's palm. "This will keep you safe. When you return, I will have an appointment for you. Our house is your house." He paused, put both hands on Juan's shoulders, and gave him a fatherly shake. "We'll dedicate a fiesta to you before you leave."

More than you know, Juan thought. Juan's heart rate returned to almost normal and he speculated that either he escaped by a hair's breadth, or this game of palace intrigue was a game he could play with impunity.

Isabella turned to leave, but Ferdinand called to her. "You've done it again. You missed a button on your gown. I'm late for a meeting with the Portuguese secretary. Juan, will you help her with that button? Thank you." The king hurried down the hall. Juan smiled, threw his shoulders back, and made a nearly inaudible laugh to Isabella as the king disappeared into the courtyard. Juan rebuttoned her gown and she called for a carriage.

Standing on the brick landing, Isabella scrutinized Juan again—a fit and dashing figure. The very essence of a court hero off to save the world. She thought it was good for her as well. The queen's carriage arrived pulled by two black horses. A page helped her into the carriage, and they rode quietly through the cobbled streets of Segovia.

Upon their arrival, the page helped the queen out of the carriage and ran to announce her presence. A priest exited the church and flowed toward Queen Isabella. The threesome then marched toward the sanctuary, the priest's robes and Isabella's gown fluttering in the mild breeze. Juan smiled and followed.

"Have you come for confession?" the priest asked, as if a previous confession that had involved Isabella and Juan foretold this occasion.

"No, we have come on an important mission. Juan is on his way to Granada to fight the Moors. I want you to give him blessings and strength for his trials ahead so that he will return to us as a new hero of our united Spain. Perhaps the holy water will help protect him."

"Bless you, my son." The priest continued for several minutes in Latin and finished with a short chant, also in Latin. Catering to the queen he knew, he said, "Holy water is good, but today we shall have wine." He poured wine into large goblets and they raised the goblets together. After a second round, he announced that the pope would be pleased that the battle in Granada would continue with even more force. The priest asked about the king. Isabella said he kept busy arguing with Portugal and trade route negotiations.

After a third round and with slurred speech, the priest told Juan that the wine was good, but it was the water that grew the grapes that made the difference. With the wine doing its usual job on the priest, he didn't notice Isabella's lustful looks into Juan's eyes or that her hands were caressing his shoulder and leg. Juan smiled a silly smile, slid his hand down her lower back, put a modest squeeze on her cheek, and nodded.

"Mind me, my son; water is your destiny. You will discover and drink from heavenly pools, and that water will mark you for infamy."

Juan's eyes widened and he nodded appropriately, trying not to giggle. Isabella smiled as she realized why she was attracted to the cute and masculine Juan. She suggested they return to the courtyard for their siestas.

For the next week, Juan accepted admonitions, blessings, and practical advice. The royal armory fitted him with armor and a royal sword. The king pronounced him ready for battle. The night before he left, Juan came to the fiesta in his high-heeled dancing boots, tight black trousers, a ruffled shirt, a red sash around his waist, and a silk vest. Isabella gasped and knew she would miss her dashing young man. Juan danced with several young ladies, as was customary. He performed well. Obviously, not all his court studies revolved around battle tactics, riding, and religion. As he turned a beautiful young lady around the floor, Isabella, at the king's side, wished she could get him away just one more time.

In the morning, a royal ceremony sent Juan off with a military escort. Days of riding south didn't dampen his enthusiasm, and Juan arrived in Granada with his contingent still intact that delivered him to General Ortega's compound. In the outer courtyard, Juan noticed a table overflowing with fresh fruit, meat, and bread. Officers escorted young ladies and helped themselves to the feast. The royal contingent left Juan alone with the general's aide. The aide guided him through a small archway where Juan produced his papers and waited for the general to review them. General Ortega entered the private courtyard from his office with the papers in hand. The general was a large man, well over six feet tall and very heavy. Juan recognized him as less than physically fit. His jowls and chin hung loosely, and he had lost any semblance of firm shape.

"So, you came by your own request to fight the holy war?"

"I am ready to fight, sir."

"Fighting, fighting, everybody wants to fight. Fighting is for those poor souls out there sleeping on the cold hard ground and eating what we throw them."

Juan stood erect, holding to his convictions. He swallowed hard and remained silent. This wasn't the military discipline he expected. Juan looked through another archway, however, and agreed the ground looked hard, a condition he had failed to consider when thoughts of thrilling victorious battle brought him here. The general's sentiments contrasted sharply with what Juan anticipated, based upon his training as a military tactician.

"You're silent. Do you have an argument for that?"

"My armor is ready, and I can handle my sword."

"Your royal sword. You can go out there with my men, risk losing your sword and your life. Then I will have to explain it to the king. Or . . . you can stay in this courtyard with me, eat well, and drink wine. I need a good tactician here with me."

Juan thought about that possibility. The table of food and the young ladies in the outer courtyard came to mind. Perhaps not all fighting involved personally sticking a sword in another man's neck. Perhaps ordering somebody else to do it was a possibility. Perhaps the glory of victory could be achieved from a higher ground. And besides, the thought of the good life, good food, and wine was appealing. "As you read, my tactical abilities are valuable." Juan thought quickly. "And, yes, yes. I think I can help you right here."

"Good." General Ortega smiled broadly, then contemplated how he would keep Juan safe, make him a disciple, then send him back to the king to sing his praises. "The guard will get you settled in and we'll review our battle strategies after breakfast."

Juan pondered his situation. He had the queen's affections, the priest blessed him with an admonition for water, the king sent him off with effective papers, and now the general prepared to reward him with praises and medals, all the while, living the good life. Juan discarded thoughts of physical battle and hardship. He thought about his fortunate plight, Oh don't worry about me, this happens to me all the time.

A hearty breakfast with well-connected officers, there mostly from court appointments, led to a strategy session with General Ortega and several other officers. The general informed the officers that Juan had high praise from his educators and credentials in battle strategies, and that he would be an aide to one of the general's assistants. Juan had slept on the idea of playing the political game he recognized before him. He made friends and asked nonthreatening questions.

Weeks later, Juan realized that the Moors were not being reinforced since all hostile routes to Granada were secured by General Ortega. Not only were the opposition forces not being reinforced, they were hopelessly out-manned, low on munitions, and hungry. Still, General Ortega was in no rush to defeat them. They served his purpose perfectly. He was living well. Letters notified the king regularly about victories. Ortega decorated his favored officers. He particularly relished receiving congratulatory documents from the king. In another year, he would crush the Moors and retire to promised landholdings with a royal endowment. Life couldn't get any better.

Life wasn't bad for Juan, either. The general promoted him twice and issued several letters of commendation for military excellence, all without Juan ever drawing his sword. Juan bided his time. He watched battles from horseback at a safe distance and studied how men fought and reacted. He analyzed the battle lines and encampments. Supply lines became an obsession because armies required food and supplies. How it all worked intrigued Juan. What he learned from the court educators was good but woefully incomplete without seeing it all first-hand. And, best of all, without bloodying his own hands.

A month after Juan's arrival, the general ordered him to head-quarters. General Ortega offered Juan a chair opposite his desk littered with maps and letters. "I am going to relieve you of your duty to Ramirez. From now on you will report to me." Before the general offered any details, an aide shouted an alarm and the general rushed out the door. In the office by himself, Juan decided to inspect the letter the general had held in his hand. Juan stood and edged next to the desk from where he could sneak a peek at the paper, being careful to not appear to be snooping if the door should suddenly reopen. Juan smiled broadly, exhaled, and repositioned himself in the chair. The letter detailed instructions for the general and was signed by the queen.

After almost a year in Granada, General Ortega consulted with Juan to organize the final battle plan to annihilate the Moors. The general prepared to make the most of his victory. He commissioned Juan to personally deliver the final battle plan to the king. The general wrote that by the time the king received Juan, the war will have ended, and that the king should feel comfortable about relaying that information to the pope in Rome. Juan gladly accepted the commission and set off with a military contingent to the court.

The king was ecstatic, and so was Isabella. Juan found himself at the right place at the right time. In short order, Juan received a new commission from the king—to train and outfit a fighting force to accompany Christopher Columbus in his quest to reach Asia by sailing west. Juan tried to work his mind around getting to the east by sailing west. It didn't make too much sense. At court, the concept created great excitement, some controversy, and some financial concerns.

Isabella rolled over and poked Juan in the ribs. "I need this Columbus venture to pay off. I need those ships to be secure. How is the training and outfitting going?"

"I've got some loyal men in good positions; they can handle themselves and more."

"We can't take any chances. It's so important, I almost want you to go, to be sure—but I don't want to lose you, either. No, I don't want you to go."

The queen's concern over Columbus's expedition consumed her even here in bed, Juan thought. Juan decided to intensify the training and request even more money for battle gear. It would cut into his leisure time, but at least he didn't have to go. Again, he considered that he would gain more by letting others do the dirty work and take the chances with their lives.

Life at the court was good until March the following year, when all life in Spain changed. The entire world changed. Columbus returned with stories of the new world, and of gold. Juan joined the royalty to hear of the discoveries. The thought of gold held everybody's attention. The thought of new lands that seemed available for the taking set imaginations running wild.

Juan knew he had to be a part of the exploitation of a new world. He knew he had to find a way to get there. How? He wasn't a sea captain, a navigator, or even a sailor. He was a military man. After all, he had trained the military for the first expedition to the new world. The quandary Juan focused on was that he didn't want to fight; he wanted an appointment.

Once again, Juan fell into an ideal position. Columbus had negotiated an extremely lucrative deal with the crown for his first voyage. The king immediately begrudged it, but he couldn't renege on it. Even the pope had approved the contract. Still, the king was resentful and didn't trust Columbus. Ferdinand needed somebody he could rely on for the next expedition.

He made Juan promises for positions in the new world. Perfect, Juan thought. Promises, but no appointment. Why was the king withholding an appointment? Without any obvious reason, Juan worried about the lack of a definite appointment. Was the king suspicious? Was he being sent to the new world to be at the discretion of Columbus? Columbus's vengeful nature came to mind as Juan recollected discussions of how

Columbus had controlled his men and the Natives of the first expedition. Juan didn't sleep well.

"Juan, the queen and I have been talking, and . . . I'm not happy."

Juan shifted his weight, hoping his knees didn't buckle. Was this it? Was his affair about to be his undoing? Juan managed to look the king in the eyes. The king's intense stare transformed into a broad smile. Juan regained his composure and smiled back.

The king continued, "We want to bestow upon you the title of Royal Conquistador. And as such, you will no longer be known as Juan, but as Conquistador Ponce de Leon. You will report directly to me, not to Christopher Columbus. Good luck in the new world. I gave Columbus too much power. I need you to represent us and our interests."

CHAPTER 2

Upon landing in the new world, Ponce watched Columbus punish the Natives for destroying the settlement he had left behind on his first voyage. Columbus began an even more serious quest for gold. European diseases made subduing the new world population a relatively easy task. The Natives had no immunity and they endured new diseases. In their suffering, Columbus set the model for subjugation in the west. Finding gold proved to be a bit more difficult without healthy Natives to work the mines, but gold they did find.

Ponce studied Columbus's tactics and found them to be very effective. Utilizing those techniques, Ponce built defensive positions, settlements, and farming operations. Within six years, Ponce had accumulated a large fortune. Columbus loaded gold onto the Spanish ships. Ponce's farming operations served more than the local community. Spanish ship captains paid handsome prices for livestock and fresh produce to provision their trip back to Spain. Ponce laughed all the way to his secret cellar to count his bars and doubloons.

The European diseases devastated the Native population, but the Natives were to exert their revenge unknowingly. Venereal diseases were endemic in the west. Sailors and sea captains carried the diseases home and their celebratory parties assured infections at all levels of society. Neither Columbus nor Ponce were immune. Strange things happened, and the doctors had no answers. Disregarding some medical discomforts, things went well for several years.

Finally, Caribs, the local population on Hispaniola, took matters into their own hands. Ponce's military training finally came in handy. The Caribs attempted a revolt. Ponce forfeited some good farmers, their families, and several neighboring Carib camps. He would have to train some new farmers, but he still had his head and his gold. When Ponce made a quick trip back to Spain, the king presented letters appointing Ponce, provisional governor. The new governor immediately realized that the gold he had accumulated was now legitimate. As governor, he was entitled to accumulate wealth. He returned to the west and practiced governorship.

Not many years later, Ponce, despite his legitimate wealth, found himself in grief upon hearing of Isabella's death. He pondered whether his trysts with the queen were safely locked in the crypt, or if she had blabbed everything on her deathbed. Letters and official documents from the court led him to believe he was home free. The king incessantly relied upon Ponce for information on new discoveries and on the doings of the Columbus family. The king had legitimate reasons to monitor the Columbus family. They were amassing wealth, stature, and power in the new lands. The king had to stay ahead of them.

Ponce decided to go home with his gold. Being well received, Ponce acted on his good fortune, which was considerable. Not only was he a favorite at court, but he had enough gold to buy some of the king's valuable farmland. Shortly after he announced the acquisition of his new farmlands, Leonora, a low-level noble lady, made a play for a place at court and on the land. Ponce found this woman quite agreeable with her favors, wit, and ambitions. He married her. By the time of the marriage, the easy life had added considerably to Ponce's girth. Even his chin had begun to sag. Nothing like General Ortega, but not the fit figure of Isabella's dream. He still had appeal to the court. Ponce lived the regal life for several years, until the king called upon him once again.

Rumors of new gold sources circulated at court— substantial gold in Puerto Rico. Ponce could have verified that. He had secretly explored the island and his men had found gold there. The king offered him a ship and fifty men to conquer Puerto Rico and secure the gold for Spain. Within a year, as governor of Puerto Rico, Ponce confiscated the easy gold and had more settlements built.

After another year in Hispaniola, the struggle between the crown and Columbus's son resulted in Ponce losing his governorship. He remained a wealthy man in Hispaniola, however, with Leonora and their family. Leonora would have preferred to be in the Spanish court, but here in the west, she built her own court and threw her own parties. Ponce was now an afterthought for her.

Ponce petitioned Leonora to throw a party with considerable political overtones. Leonora agreed. She spared no expense to decorate the courtyard with brilliant flowers on every wall. The best musicians played deep into the night. All the important European families of the islands convened. The most important guests were the Columbus family. Courtly demeanor pervaded every corner; none of the families would dare to breach political conformities, despite wine flowing freely.

As the music blared and the candles blazed, Columbus's son, who was becoming a power in the islands and beyond, spoke with Ponce away from the crowd. "You have put on a fantastic fiesta. We will reciprocate soon. We will have a good time."

"The king would be proud to be here."

Columbus's son turned and marched back to refill his cup. At that point, Ponce knew he had succeeded. The Columbuses had been delivered the message that the king still had influence in the conquered west.

A few more years passed, and the king had given in to some of Ponce's rivals. Ponce returned to Spain and told the king he preferred to stay there. Ferdinand balked at the suggestion. The king envisioned vast new lands and wealth. They negotiated.

"I need you over there," Ferdinand said.

"What more can I do there?" Ponce asked.

"I've heard you discussing the fountain everlasting. And besides, what can you do here?"

"I can raise bulls on my rancho grande."

"You can take some of my bulls with you, and being governor for life . . ." The king reached for and scratched his crotch. "I'd like to catch the son of a bitch that gave that disease to the queen before she died. The doctors are fairly sure the sailors are bringing it back from the Natives over there."

Ponce shook his head in condolence. He had the same urges to scratch and knew how the king felt about it. He could never admit that he too carried the disease.

"What were you about to say about a governorship?"

"Oh yeah. If you'll go on the mission for Spain, you can take a small herd and have the governorship of all the territories on the mainland." The king continued to scratch.

"Well, I guess I better prepare for a major mission then."

In exchange for conquering new lands in the name of Spain, Ponce would hold the exclusive rights to the governorship for life. That much effort sounded like real work. But Ponce had seized upon the rumors of the Fountain of Youth. The Spaniards had no concept that they weren't in Asia, and everybody knew the Fountain of Youth was in Asia. Ponce pondered the thought. Perhaps the Fountain of Youth could be over there.

Then, Ponce focused on the admonition the priest issued before he set off for Granada. Could he drink from the Fountain of Youth? Yes!

This was his destiny. This is the water he was groomed to discover. More than gold, more than the power of the governorship, finding the fabled Fountain of Youth set Ponce's heart aflutter. Forever he would be the most famous man in the world. He would build a monument in his name at the fountain. He would be more important than any general, conquistador, or king. He would even rival the pope. And the king would pay for the entire enterprise. And . . . the king would never suspect him of infecting the queen.

Ponce had all the money and wealth he could ever spend. But the idea of untold fame pushed him over the edge. He accepted the king's offer, marshaled his forces, and set off to a land he would call Florida.

From Puerto Rico, Ponce ventured forth and landed three ships and two hundred men on the east coast of Florida. Finding little of interest other than the land, he returned to Puerto Rico, which was in chaos. He left again for Spain. In Spain, the king reaffirmed him governor of Florida and Bimini and ordered him to bring peace to Puerto Rico by killing everybody necessary. Ponce muddled in the war until King Ferdinand died. Then, because it was more important than fighting, Ponce returned to Spain to consolidate his wealth and position. Being assured everything continued in his favor, Ponce returned to the quest for the Fountain of Youth. On his second expedition, he landed one ship with his men plus a supply ship far up on the western shores of Florida.

Ponce's ship with soldiers, personal possessions, and weapons anchored in the pristine bay; nearby, the supply ship with food supplies and horses anchored and waited for orders. Immediately, Ponce knew he was onto something good. With the ship safely anchored, Ponce scanned the area. He noticed the small clear-water river running into the bay. Ponce's men rowed a small boat ashore. Ponce stood in the bow as the boat neared the beach. He made quite the impression in his red cape, shiny armor breastplate, and polished helmet. As they stood on a fine-white-sand beach with lush flowering bushes at the edges of the sand, a Native man met him sporting a very large gold nugget aligned on a necklace with many pieces of seashells. Ponce pointed to his ships and then to an area at the south end of the beach. With some gestures he indicated that he wanted to set up a camp. The Native man shrugged and left. Being of European descent, Ponce assumed that the Native agreed; after all, almost everybody agreed, given the thuggish force available. Ponce then ordered the supply ship to transport the supplies and horses ashore. Even with calm waters, the horses were stressed before they set foot on the white sands of Florida. He ordered his men to construct a fortified position down the beach. When the beach was littered with crates of supplies, Ponce waved off the supply vessel. He was glad to be rid of the stench from the ugly ship.

Ponce's men set up a temporary position that would protect the men, horses, and supplies. Each day the compound grew, and farming operations commenced almost immediately. Interactions with the Native population remained minimal until the Spaniards revealed themselves and ventured onto the open beach. Ponce ordered his intelligence officer to teach the Natives to speak their Spanish. The intelligence officer wasn't all that intelligent, but he had learned to communicate with Natives in Hispaniola and Puerto Rico. It didn't occur to Ponce that without learning the Native language, he would be vulnerable. But after all, brute force had always worked in the west so far.

The Spaniards fortified their small settlement and expanded their farming operations. Natives made occasional visits, and quickly the language barrier dissolved. Even with modest communication skills, the Natives avoided providing Ponce the source of the gold pieces they wore around their necks. Ponce and his lieutenants avoided threats but attempted to determine the source of gold.

Ponce's second in command noticed one of his men with a piece of gold about the size of the end of his little finger. He brought the low-level soldier before Ponce.

"How did you come to that gold?" Ponce asked.

"I traded for it," the soldier said.

"What did you trade?"

"A sea snail."

"A snail? Where did you get it?" Ponce asked, demanding an immediate answer.

"I was diving in the lagoon over there. When I carried the shell onto the beach, an Indian wearing the gold piece asked me what I was going to do with it. I figured he wanted it, so I played hard to get. He offered me water. I said no. Then he opened his bag and pulled out several polished shells. I looked at them and said no. I pointed to his gold piece. He took it off and handed it to me."

"Trading? What a novel idea." That set Ponce to thinking down a different path. If I can get the gold for snails that are free for the taking, why get bogged down with mining operations? I can live the easy life right here on the beach and collect all the gold with no problems. Then we'll find the Fountain of Youth.

Ponce slept on it and in the morning sought out the chief to verify the snails' value to the Indians. Manchun, a tall and handsome man that appeared to be in his mid-thirties, agreed to meet Ponce on the beach. Ponce asked about Manchun's status. Manchun told him he controlled all the people and land from the bay to the north for a long way. Manchun in no way actually considered that he controlled the people in this area. He had friends and relatives that respected him. But for purposes of this conversation, it put him on an equal footing with this stranger. In a coy beat-around-the-bush style, Ponce made small talk before he ever mentioned snails. He carefully studied the chief's reaction when he brought it up. The chief gave a little smile and shrugged. Not entirely as enthusiastic as Ponce had hoped. Ponce was unaware of the conversation Manchun had with his inner circle, including the man that traded the gold. It had gone something like this:

"We can have conch tonight," the young man said as he presented the live conch to the chief, Manchun.

"You had a good dive," Manchun said.

"No, a Spaniard dove and brought it up. He offered it to me for a small piece of gold."

"They'd give anything for that worthless stuff," Gurefin said.

"Maybe we can parlay that desire into a grand feast without diving," said Petnima, a woman with multiple colored flowers in her hair.

"Maybe more than a feast," the chief said.

"Let's not give too much away until we know how far we can carry this," Gurefin said.

"Good point. Spread the word. Hold back any gold until we know what it's worth to them. I'll wait until they bring it up."

Ponce continued talking to Manchun and asked about gold in the area. Manchun told him there were no mines in the immediate area, but that they often had access to gold. Ponce asked about that access. Manchun shrugged, then quickly shifted the conversation from gold to snails. Manchun told him they were called conch and that he valued them, both to eat and for the shells. He added that only fresh conch from the sea had real value.

"One of my men traded a conch for a piece of gold about this big," Ponce said, displaying the end of his little finger.

"He made a bad deal. And I would remind you, your Spaniard was possibly diving in our fishery."

"How many conchs is a piece of gold like that worth?"

Manchun looked to the sea and pondered the question. "Oh, I would say maybe four or five conchs would be a fair trade. If you dive in water away from this beach." Manchun knew that for five conch shells, he could trade for ten times that much gold.

"How can we work out a trade deal?" Ponce asked.

"We would have to schedule delivery so we can plan a feast. We only eat fresh conch. They're no good if they're not fresh."

"Let us see what we can do. Can we dive around that point, on the other side of the mountain?"

"Yes, that would be okay with us." Manchun knew the conch lived in the bay over the hill. He also knew stingrays and occasionally sharks inhabited that water, but that wasn't his problem.

Ponce left the chief and returned to his partially defended settlement. An order went out for five strong swimmers to meet at the plaza in the morning. Seven candidates, including the man that traded the conch, showed up for the parlay in the plaza. Ponce hefted a conch shell and announced that they were about to embark on a new strategy to secure the gold of the area.

"The Indians will trade their gold for these sea snails they call conch. If this works out, we don't have to engage in any mining operations or do any fighting. We'll go slow to see how this goes. You're going to climb over that mountain, dive in the bay and pick these snails from the sea floor. The chief wants to know when they will arrive so they can arrange a fiesta-type meal."

"How many do they want?"

"I'll let you know. Any more questions?" Ponce released his men to daily chores.

Meanwhile, in a glen with a small crystal-clear river running through it, Manchun briefed his people in the shade of lush tall trees.

"These Spaniards are willing to work for gold. They want to trade fresh conch for some of the gold the northern tribes have traded to us for the conch shells. I think Ponce is about to make a deal. All we must do is to keep them away from the northern tribes."

"We should test them first. Let's see if they can dive. Then we'll see how greedy they are," Petnima said.

"I told them that we would need four or five conchs for another piece of gold that size. They're going to dive in the bay on the other side of the mountain."

"I want to watch them fish," Gurefin said.

"I can imagine it could be interesting. When they come to me I'll tell them we'll try the conchs, and we'll have a party." The economic picture looked rosy. Manchun and his people would continue to trade conch shells for gold from the northern tribes. The Spaniards would trade live conchs for gold. The Manchun contingency would enjoy fine dining and would manage the trade center as it developed.

Two days later, Ponce sent an emissary to ask for a meeting on the beach at the mouth of the river. Manchun agreed to meet Ponce when the sun was high overhead, which would be in about two hours.

"Why do you want to have a meeting in the hot sun?" Gurefin asked Manchun.

"I'll be dressed for it, like this." He slapped his bare chest and pointed to his thigh-length shorts and bare feet. "He'll probably wear his armor and his clumsy boots, not good in the sand."

Gurefin and Petnima laughed out loud. "We'll have a little fun with them while we can," Petnima said.

"Can you imagine what it's like, wearing all that all that shiny gear in the sun?" Gurefin said.

"Yes, but be careful. If we ever find it necessary to fight them, that stuff will give them the advantage. For now, we'll have an edge in negotiating," Manchun said.

"Not very good camouflage."

"No, but they've got those guns and steel swords."

"Doesn't give them any advantage while they're diving for conchs," Petnima said.

Ponce and his entourage, dressed to the hilt, trudged through the sand to meet Manchun and his friends.

"Your costumes are impressive," Manchun said.

"Thank you, we find them very useful at times," Ponce said, in a stiff-lipped kind of way, not realizing the irony of Manchun's mention of costumes.

"How are your gardens growing? Well, I hope," Gurefin asked.

"The soils are good. The crops are doing nicely."

Manchun took a step back and stared at the four Spaniards in full armor, shiny body shields, helmets, long swords, heavy boots, and long red capes. "We've never had dress like that here."

"Like I said, it comes in handy at times."

Manchun recognized some discomfort in the Spaniards' faces and stiff upright stances. They shifted their weight and he noticed perspiration dripping into their beards from under the helmets. He decided to let them swelter a while longer. "Tell us about your homes. I understand they are far away."

Ponce smiled broadly at the opportunity to brag about all the features of a royal civilization. He described large homes, roads, castles, fences, wealth, and all that wealth could buy. The perspiration changed to heavy sweat running down his face and into his eyes and black beard. With the description of the royal castle, Ponce stopped, removed his helmet, and wiped his brow. His men followed the example. Finally, with his helmet tucked under his arm, he asked about gold.

"We have some gold."

"What do you use it for?" Ponce asked.

"We wear it sometimes," Manchun answered.

"Where do you mine it?"

"We don't dig in the dirt for it."

"Where do you get it?"

"We have friends—some far away."

"Will you trade some gold for conchs?"

"Do you think you can catch them?"

"One of my men caught one. He said we could get more."

"Okay."

"We will trade three conchs for gold the size you gave my man for the first one."

"No. My nephew made a bad deal."

Ponce stiffened. He didn't expect a negotiation. Ponce didn't understand. After all, this was just a barefoot Native. He didn't speak Latin, didn't belong to his church, and certainly had not been educated at court. Who did he think he was negotiating with? No one should question a royal expedition leader, a conquistador, especially not a governor.

Ponce's armor shined brightly in the sun. The armor's surface temperature also rose substantially. Ponce and his men were uncomfortable. This had to end. He stood silent, then he wiped his brow and asked, "How about four, then?"

Manchun immediately said, "No."

"We talked about four or five, I thought."

"Then why were you talking about three?"

Ponce didn't have much of an answer for that and remained silent. It seemed being a Spaniard in full conquistador dress didn't carry that much weight here on the beach. But it carried plenty of heat.

"Now it's five."

Ponce shifted his weight from one leg to the other and dropped his helmet in the sand. He left it there. Pretending not to notice. "Okay, five."

"Five and we'll make the trade, but . . . they must be fresh from the sea. If even one is not fresh—no gold."

"Okay," Ponce said and stooped to retrieve his helmet.

"You must tell us when you will bring them, so we can plan to eat them fresh. Only fresh."

"Let's meet right here at this time the day after tomorrow. We'll have the conchs."

"We'll bring a piece of gold."

The Spaniards repositioned their helmets and began the laborious trek off the beach. The remaining sand in Ponce's helmet irritated his partially bald head but he refused to acknowledge it to anybody watching. Manchun and Gurefin retreated to the shade of tall trees and into the bushes to their camp in the glen by the clear-water river. Several friends, who had been watching from the bushes, joined them.

"Why would anyone wear a getup like that to the beach in full sun?" Gurefin asked.

"I guess they thought they made a point. Weren't you impressed?" Petnima asked.

"Oh yes, yes I was—at stupidity," Manchun answered. They all had a hearty laugh. "No wonder they like it here, given their description of where they came from. Do you think they were bragging or complaining?"

"Who would want to live in a castle? No clean water, fresh food, or sanitation. It must be a dirty, dark, and smelly place," Petnima said. "Not like our hall of plenty, a land with flowers, where we can come and go as we please."

"We're okay for now; the numbers are on our side. But remember the stories we've heard about their activities on some of the islands. They're not to be trusted. Does anybody want to go over to the bay and watch them dive?" Manchun asked.

"I want to go see if they can swim in those outfits," Targonsa said.

"Okay, Targonsa. You go and tell us about their adventure."

On the designated morning, Targonsa trotted up a circuitous trail to the top of the small mountain and took a seat overlooking the bay below. He watched five Spaniards leave their compound with machetes to hack their way through the dense foliage, including jasmine, columbine, and flowering shrubs that bloomed beneath the palms. A straight-line path to the singular destination was their only goal. Targonsa would have followed a more indirect course with established trails and smelled the flowers, which would have assured a faster and safer trip. But there they were, hacking and destroying some of the most beautiful plants they'd ever seen. Once on the beach, they stripped down and waded into the azure bay.

In shoulder-depth water, they began to dive. They came up empty, apparently aware that they would have to swim into a deeper part of the bay, dive, and ferry their prizes back to shore. After diving deep, a diver came up with a conch and alerted his fellow divers. He swam with the conch and deposited it on the beach. A second diver also found success. They continued to dive without more success and decided to take a rest on the beach; after all, the beach offered the softest, whitest sand they had ever seen. While on the beach, one of them found a conch that had washed up onto shore; he carried it back to the others.

"Put it in the pile. We need all we can get. That's a hard swim, all the way out there."

"Let's get two more and get out of here."

They swam back into deep water and searched for almost thirty minutes until they miraculously discovered that the conchs inhabited a specific area off the north shore. They picked two and swam back to the beach. Five conchs fulfilled their orders. They lounged on the beach before they made their way back through the wilted and withering flowers they had hacked down.

A pleased smile spread over Ponce's face. He thanked the divers and told them to pick up a bottle of wine for their efforts. Ponce ordered two men to dress in semi-beach casual—open-necked long-sleeved shirts, full-length trousers, and sandals. No swords, capes, or helmets. They gathered the conchs and headed for the beach.

Manchun and friends, including Targonsa, watched them enter the beach while they waited in the shade of palm trees on the opposite end of the beach. When the Spaniards reached the agreed-upon area, Manchun called out and waved, "Over here in the shade."

Targonsa turned to Petnima, smiled, and tried not to laugh out loud. The Spaniards were halfway to appropriate beach wear.

One of Ponce's escorts said, "That makes sense."

Ponce led his aides into the shade. "We have the conchs," he announced proudly.

"Yes, and we have the gold. Did you have a good swim?" Manchun asked.

"The men didn't complain."

Manchun took that statement with a grain of salt. He knew nobody would complain to the master conquistador. "Let's have a look."

Ponce motioned for his men to open the bag and display the conchs. Manchun picked one up and rolled it over. He handed it to Targonsa. He did the same with the second and the third snail. Ponce smiled at the anticipation of the gold. Manchun picked up the fourth conch, rolled it over and stared at the discolored fleshy foot.

"No good. This one's not fresh. You picked this from the beach."

"What do you mean? How can you tell?" Ponce demanded.

Manchun picked up the fifth conch. "Look. Compare the color. See, this one is fresh. The foot is pink. This one from the beach is gray. It's no good. No gold today."

"My men worked hard for those. We expect a smaller piece of gold for the four good ones."

"No gold. The deal was five fresh conchs, not four and a sick one." Manchun decided to see how desperate the Spaniards were for gold. "Do you want to try again?"

"We want to get paid for four."

"We want you to live up to your agreements. You, as a man, agreed to the deal. Five conchs or no gold."

Ponce resented a challenge to his manhood, but he knew he was wrong. In any other setting he would have expected to be called on it. He didn't expect it from this Native in the new world. He turned his back on Manchun and the rest. He didn't like being in this uncomfortable situation. He could just leave. He could argue, but he would be arguing against what he knew was right. How could the predicament be put back upon Manchun's shoulders? He couldn't reason it out. He himself had created the situation.

The remaining participants from both parties smiled at each other and used body and facial gestures, not visible to Ponce, to question what Ponce would do. Finally, Ponce turned and rejoined the discussion. With a frown and in a grave voice, Ponce told Manchun they would be back the next day with five fresh conchs. He motioned for his men to follow him. Ponce's reputation depended on delivering five conchs. Ponce didn't even give consideration to keeping the conchs he didn't get paid for. If he had thought about it, he would have kept them. Being put in his place precluded any other negotiations. He simply wanted to leave.

When the Spaniards disappeared, Gurefin said, "We've got four good conchs."

"And an extra shell," Manchun said.

"Let's eat," Petnima said.

By the time Ponce had settled himself with a cup of wine, he had decided not to punish his men. He called for the divers and told them they must dive in the morning and come back with five fresh conchs. He made it crystal clear that only the snails alive in the sea were acceptable. He explained how to check the flesh color for freshness and sent them off.

As the sun rose, Targonsa watched the five Spanish divers trudge over their trail of wilted flowers to the beach. They carefully waded toward the deep water. When they were in water just over their waists, the diver second in line yelled that something had bitten him. They carried him out onto the beach to inspect his leg. There appeared to be a small wound just above his ankle that caused great pain. The divers had no idea whether the wound would prove to be deadly, but they were assured by the victim that it was painful. They carried him back to the compound.

Targonsa ran back to Manchun to report that a diver had been stung by a stingray. Petnima said he would get over it. The Spaniards had never encountered a stingray and probably had no concept of effective treatment. Manchun thought for a moment and decided to convince the Spaniards that they had some magical powers of their own. "Bring a jar of water. We'll refer to it as our 'pure water.' Let's go see how he's doing."

Manchun, Gurefin, and Targonsa went to the Spanish compound. They told the guard they knew a diver was injured and that they might be able to save him. The guard told them to wait while he ran to inform Ponce and the divers. Ponce told him to bring the Natives. In the compound, Ponce's doctor looked at the wound but did little else. Manchun told the doctor he could possibly save him and relieve the pain. The diver gasped, "Yes, the pain; stop the pain!" Manchun told them to bring hot water and something to wrap his leg. The doctor ordered the hot water. When the hot water arrived, Manchun ceremoniously took the jar from Targonsa and poured half of it into the hot water.

"This is some of our pure water. It can save lives," Manchun said. He took the cloth and soaked it in the hot water and applied the compress over the wound. He touched the diver's leg below his knee and asked if it hurt.

"Not there," the diver answered, and continued to writhe in pain.

"We'll keep this hot pure water on it for a while." Manchun continued to soak the compress in the hot water and alternately pressed it firmly over the wound. He told the doctor to keep the water hot. The doctor's helper took the jar and placed it over the fire. By the time Manchun applied the third compress, the contorted look on the diver's face had begun to dissipate. Manchun kept hot compresses on the wound for over an hour.

"How's the pain now?" Manchun asked.

"Not as bad. Could I have died?"

"It can happen."

Ponce arrived and asked the doctor about his diver. The doctor told him Manchun had alleviated the pain and possibly saved his life by mixing his pure water with hot water and applying it to the wound.

"What bit him?" Ponce asked.

"It wasn't a bite. A poison dart on the tail of a stingray got him," Gurefin said.

"We didn't see anything in the water before he got hit," another diver said.

"You wouldn't see them unless you scared them away before they sting you. They sleep just under the sand."

"How often do you get stung?" the diver asked.

"We don't get stung. We scare them away or swim over them."

"How do you scare them away?"

"We shuffle our feet in the sand, or we use a stick to disturb the sand."

"What did you pour into the hot water?" the doctor asked.

"Some of our pure water," Manchun answered.

"Pure water?" the doctor asked.

"Yes. It's good for a lot of things. It's especially good for neutralizing poison. It helps keep us healthy and young."

That got Ponce's attention. "How does it keep you young?" Ponce asked.

"How old do you think I am?" Manchun asked.

"About thirty-five," Ponce answered.

Manchun smiled and shook his head. "I am not the leader here because of my youth."

Ponce's eyes lit up. Quite serendipitously, he was discussing the subject of his quest. Gold and conchs were immaterial now. "Where do you get it?"

"Far away. Up north. We go there twice a year to camp near the source. We drink the water and carry as much back as we can."

"How far north?" Ponce asked.

"Many days."

"Will you take us there?"

"There's no gold there, just water."

"Yes, will you take us there?" Ponce anxiously asked.

Manchun had him hooked. Did he really believe in pure water? Why was it more valuable than gold? Now he had something the Spaniards wanted even more than gold. Unbelievable, Manchun thought. He didn't answer but went back to work on his patient.

Ponce decided quickly that he couldn't afford to offend the source of information that would fulfill his quest. He fully intended to cajole Manchun into an invitation. He believed there would be a better time. Ponce backed off and thanked Manchun for saving his diver.

Manchun asked Ponce if he still wanted to dive for conchs. Ponce said now that they knew how to avoid the stingrays, they would try it again. Gurefin told him that if the sharks came back, they should stay out of the water. Ponce told him they knew better than to swim with sharks.

Manchun told the doctor to continue to apply the hot compresses until the pain disappeared and the diver would be okay. As he prepared to leave, Manchun told Ponce to let him know when they wanted to trade five fresh conchs for the gold.

Back in the glen under the trees and by the small river, Targonsa began to laugh. Manchun sat facing him and smiled back. Gurefin was the first to speak. "We've got to get some more of that pure water."

"It's very valuable and rare; remind me to dip some more out of the river."

"What are you talking about?" Petnima asked.

"Manchun convinced the Spaniards that our water has magical powers. They believe it saved their diver from certain death after a stingray got him," Targonsa said.

"That's crazy. Everybody knows all you do is apply heat to keep the poison local. It cures itself," Petnima said.

"They don't know that," Manchun said.

"Talk about gullible," Gurefin said.

"They want to believe it. Remember how they tried to convert us to their religion? Blind faith. There's no basis. Create an answer and conjure questions that make it happen," Manchun said.

"We should always be ready to offer answers and let them formulate their own questions. It will be fun watching them defy logic to make what they want to believe true in their minds," Gurefin said.

"What are you going to do about taking them to the source of the water?" Targonsa asked.

"I don't know. For now, we'll stall them. It sure seemed like it's important to them. If they believe we've got it and they don't, we've got a lever. Maybe we should march them up to the Vortex. The problem is, I don't know what we'd do with them after that. Sooner or later, even they would conclude that it was just water."

"We've got enough to keep them on the edge for now," Gurefin said.

Several days passed in the pleasant weather with blue skies and warm sea breezes. The Spaniards worked in their gardens and fortified the walls around their compound. The Natives killed an alligator and enjoyed barbecued gator tail on the beach while they relished the sunsets and comfort of the calm bay.

The following week, Ponce sent a messenger to Manchun to set a trade date involving the conchs and the gold. Manchun told him the next day would be good. The messenger set the time and place before he marched back to the compound.

Bright and early, five divers, including the diver that had been stung, made their way back to the bay carrying sticks to help chase any stingrays away. They stood at the water's edge and considered what else in the water could hurt them. They didn't see any evidence of sharks and found the courage to venture forth. The sticks churned the sand mercilessly before the divers without incident. Targonsa laughed at the commotion the nervous Spaniards produced in the sand, not wanting to risk another sting. They began their swim in waist-deep water.

Bringing in a conch created another problem, however. Without a stick, the first diver appeared to trip the light fantastic as he shuffled his feet in the sand. With the conch safely in the bag, the diver shuffled his feet back into deep water for another try. Before long, they had their five fresh conchs and made their way to the compound.

Ponce inspected the conchs and commandeered four men to accompany him to the palms at the opposite end of the beach. A Native boy noticed the Spaniards marching in the sand and ran to alert the elders. Manchun and Targonsa met the Spaniards under the palms. "How was the dive today?" Targonsa asked.

"No stingray and we've got the five fresh conchs," Ponce answered.

Manchun inspected the conchs and approved. He motioned for Targonsa to hand over the gold. Ponce accepted the nugget and nodded his head in agreement. "Do you want some more soon?" he asked.

"We can only eat so many. Maybe in seven days we would take five more."

Ponce assumed the close and said they would deliver five more in seven days. Manchun shrugged and looked to Targonsa. Targonsa told Manchun they would be going up the river soon, but that they could leave after the next meal. Manchun said they would accept five more. Ponce thanked them and began the trek back across the beach with his gold.

Manchun chuckled and asked Targonsa what trip up the river he was talking about. Targonsa said he didn't know, but the mention of it would give the Spaniards something to think about. Manchun credited Targonsa for his quick and devious wit. He added that maybe they would disappear for a few days or more.

Back at the compound, Ponce rolled the nugget in his fingers. Rodriguez, Gomez, and Juarez sat with him at a table in the shade. Rodriguez, who Ponce relied on as his treasurer, asked Ponce if he wanted the nugget weighed, registered, and stowed on the ship.

"Yes, of course. Take care of it. The ship should always be the secure repository. Make sure it is always fully stocked as well."

"That gold and the rest of it as it comes in," Juarez, Ponce's second in command, said.

"We'll get another one before they leave," Ponce said.

"Leave? Where are they going?" Juarez asked.

"I don't know. They said they were going up the river on a trip."

"Do you think they're getting more gold, so they don't have to dive for their conchs?" Juarez asked.

"Most of them are still wearing some gold," Gomez said.

"We'll probably get some more gold, but I want to find the source of the water," Ponce said.

"We've got water here. I want the gold. My contract says I get ten percent of the gold, and I want it," Juarez said.

"You'll get your ten percent."

"Ten percent of that one nugget isn't what I signed up for."

"You signed up as my second in command; remember that. Remember what their pure water did for Jorge when he got stung."

"Yeah, well I don't intend to get stung," Juarez said as he crossed his arms and sat back from the table, dropping the subject—at least for now.

"But the water may cure some other problems as well," Gomez said, hoping to placate and gain favor with Ponce.

"I'm sure it's good for a lot. Manchun doesn't look a day over thirty-five," Ponce said. Nobody bothered to make the point that Manchun didn't actually tell them how old he was. Ponce told Rodriguez to have the divers get five more conchs in seven days, then he dismissed the group.

Manchun worked with Gurefin and Petnima to prepare the conchs for a big meal. "I think the Spaniards are convinced the water saved their diver. I think they even believe it keeps me young. We should find some more things our pure water is good for."

"How about curing the irritations from poison ivy and sumac?" Petnima asked.

"That's great. Just put the juice from bark we use into a jar, pour in some pure water, and pour out some more magic. They'll be convinced it's the water," Gurefin said.

"All we have to do is be positive about it; make them believe we believe it. Let's set it up and test it," Manchun said.

"I'll put some of our potion in a jar and have it ready—next to a jar of our pure water," Gurefin said.

"They once asked me about exploring up the coast. Maybe I'll take them up there for a day or two and expose them to some bad plants. When they show symptoms, I'll bring them back for a magical treatment," Manchun said.

Seven days passed peacefully, and Ponce, accompanied by four men, once again tread to the palms and the waiting Natives. Manchun inspected the conchs and told Ponce his divers were doing a good job. He passed the second nugget to Ponce and took the opportunity to put their most recent plan into operation.

CHAPTER 4

"One of your men once asked about making a short trip up the coast. Does he still want to go?"

"Yes. We'd like to explore more of what's up north."

"I'm going to make a two- or three-day trip on the coastline. Do your men want to come?"

"I can send four men with you."

"Good. We'll leave the day after tomorrow."

"My men will be ready."

Two days later, Manchun and Rentrani walked out onto the beach with walking sticks and small bags of essentials and watched four Spaniards approach with two horses loaded with supplies. Manchun gave them the bad news: the horses wouldn't be able to negotiate the route up the coast. Swampy areas, alligators, and rocky outcroppings made the use of horses impractical. The Spaniards returned to the compound and scaled down to supplies they were able to carry. When they returned to the beach, they were in heavy boots, full-length clothes, heavy packs, and guns. Manchun turned his back and whispered to Rentrani. Rentrani laughed.

"We're only going to be gone two or three days."

"We'll be okay," Juarez said.

Manchun led the way into a trail that paralleled the beach about two hundred yards inland. Manchun and Rentrani, with sandals, shorts, and loose-fitting shirts, looked forward to several miles in the warm and humid air. Juarez and the other Spaniards, less so. Two hours at a quick pace got them to a lush swampy area with flowering vines hanging from wide-branched trees, flowers of all colors, and to complete the picture . . . alligators, sunbathing close to the water. The Spaniards, with sweat rolling off their faces that soaked their clothes, wondered where this would lead. Juarez was concerned about the alligators. Rentrani told him they would parallel the water and alligators down to the mouth where the shallow swamp waters met the ocean, then they would wade across. Juarez wanted to know why the alligators wouldn't be at the mouth. Rentrani calmly told him that most alligators stayed away from the salt water.

Safely over the water at the edge of the ocean, they climbed a steep and jagged rock face and then scrambled down the tall outcropping back to the beach. After that, Manchun asked Juarez if he would like to take a break. The Spaniards didn't hesitate; they dropped their backpacks and flopped down on the sand in the shade of tall coconut palm trees. Rentrani told them they would follow the shoreline for the rest of the day. During their extended break, the Spaniards removed their heavy shirts and cut off the lower part of their trouser legs, trying to emulate the hiking wear of the Natives. Their backpacks, heavy boots, and long guns were still a burden, but they persisted. Late in the afternoon, Manchun chose a campsite at the edge of a small shallow bay.

Rentrani started a small fire and joined Manchun in collecting oysters and mussels to barbeque. The Spaniards built a lean-to and covered it with a tarp from one of the packs. They built a larger fire and unpacked their cookware. A heavy iron pot heated water to make stew from vegetables and dried meat. Manchun and Rentrani placed the oysters and mussels on stones near the coals and offered the Spaniards some of the delicacies. Momentarily, the fresh seafood aroma took Juarez back to his childhood in a poor seaside village in Spain. They accepted, and very much preferred the fresh seafood over their own meal of wilted vegetables and tough meat.

The Spaniards had a hard time admitting the Natives' preparation and knowledge allowed them to coexist with local conditions much more effectively than they were able to do. A light rain in the middle of the night left the Spaniards' camp supplies and equipment heavy with moisture and difficult to pack. With sour faces, they got it done and indicated they were ready to move out.

The Spaniards struggled with the rough trail that ascended into higher mountains. From atop a ridge, a spectacular view greeted them. They looked down to the ocean in the west. To the east, a large lake was alive with birds. A study of the water revealed that the lake water exited its confines over a small waterfall. The resulting river ran through the ravine below them and flowed into the ocean. Juarez studied the steep cliffs of the ravine that the river had ravaged over millennium. It reminded him of a spot in Puerto Rico where he had forced the Natives to dig gold for him.

"Have you ever been down there?" Juarez asked.

"No reason to. We're going around that and the lake," Manchun answered.

Always suspicious, especially when it came to anything about gold, Juarez questioned Manchun's quick and positive answer. "I want to go down there to inspect it more closely."

"You can go down there now, but Rentrani and I must meet some people tonight. We're going to continue. We can meet you here on our way back or we can all stop here on the way back."

Juarez thought about that. His greed for gold made the decision for him. "We'll stop here for today. Will you be back tomorrow?"

"Yes. We'll meet you here tomorrow at midday."

"Okay. We'll see you tomorrow." Juarez directed his men to organize a dry camp. He left one man to build the camp while he led two men into the canyon. No trails existed to ease their descent. They scrambled down rough rock faces and through brush and bushes. They slid down loose dirt and rocks with only minor concerns for their return. Juarez stopped several times to dig into the earth. None of his efforts revealed anything resembling gold-bearing minerals. On the canyon floor, Juarez dug into the river's gravel for placer gold. Nothing, not even black sand. The men sat near the water, drank, and stared up to the light above the canyon walls. They used bushes, grass clumps, rock outcroppings, and anything else available to aid their ascent. They did not enjoy camp, dinner, or sleep later that evening, as skin irritations persisted.

Manchun and Rentrani had continued toward the lake quietly until they could speak freely. "I don't know what they expect to discover down there. The only thing they'll find is poison ivy and sumac. They won't be able to carry enough water up from the river to help the irritation much. Their own stubbornness will take them into the evil plants. We won't have to lead them into it on the way back."

"By the time we get home, their arms and legs should be alive from those canyon plants," Rentrani said.

"I'm sure you're correct. Gurefin's potion with the pure water should convince them the water is magical. I can't wait."

Manchun and Rentrani circumnavigated the lake and hiked over a range of hills that overlooked lush meadows with tall grasses blowing in the breeze. Manchun scanned the area and told Rentrani the Spaniards would rather have been here than down that ravine. Rentrani responded that the Spaniards' agendas didn't make much sense. Manchun and Rentrani followed a trail to the small end of the nearest meadow where their friends maintained a small camp nestled within flowering vines and protective trees.

"Welcome Manchun, you're right on time. We're cooking frog legs for you tonight," Mosteen said.

"Sounds good. Is everything okay up here?"

"Good as ever. How are you doing with the Spaniards?"

"As you've heard, we're having a little fun with them."

"Are they completely helpless?"

"They're clumsy. They're greedy. They're gullible. BUT, I don't trust them. They can use brute force. They have guns, swords, and as we've heard, they don't mind using them to take what they want. That seems to be gold. It may also include the source of the pure water you heard about."

"I laughed all night when I heard about how you convinced them the water fixed the diver."

"It was worth a laugh. But you be careful. If they go crazy on us, we could be in trouble. Four of them came up with us. They wanted to explore the ravine. I think they believe there's gold down there."

Mosteen laughed. "The only thing in that ravine is poison ivy and sumac."

"I know. We're planning to help them when we get back. Gurefin has our potion in a jar. We'll ceremoniously add some water and fix the irritations. That should assure them that we have something special."

"Wish I could be there."

"Spread the word. Don't let the Spaniards catch any of our people in large groups. We should always be able to disperse, hide, and go where they will never dare follow."

"I'll let everybody know."

"Let's eat," a voice from across the campsite called.

They savored frog legs, greens, and boiled grains. Manchun shared stories with his friends around the fire late into the night. After breakfast, Manchun emptied a bag of polished shells and told Mosteen that perhaps he could trade them to the northern tribes for gold. Manchun reminded Mosteen that the Spaniards would do almost anything for gold. He accepted a bag full of grain and prepared to leave.

Back on the ridge, Juarez and two of his men were uncomfortable due to irritations on their arms and legs. The man that had stayed in camp seemed to be okay. Their packs were loaded, and they were anxious to leave.

"Find anything interesting down there?" Rentrani asked.

"No, just the river," Juarez answered. He held his arm up and then pointed to his legs. "How long will this irritation last?"

"Usually three or four days. We'll get some pure water on it as soon as we get back."

"Let's keep moving, then."

The group traveled all day, climbed the rocky ridge, and crossed the river at the mouth. By the time they made camp for the evening, the sweat on the irritated skin made life almost unbearable. They broke camp early and spent the morning trekking in misery, getting to the home beach by midmorning. Rentrani made a commotion, conjuring an emergency. He called for someone in the camp to bring some pure water. Gurefin yelled back. Other Natives ran onto the beach. It was a planned response, but the Spaniards took it as an unusual emergency. The guards at Ponce's settlement recognized something going on and raised an alarm. Ponce and three armed men came onto the beach. He recognized Juarez with his men and hurried across the sand to get more information.

Gurefin met Juarez and the men on the beach. He held a large jar. "I will pour this pure water on one arm. Rub it in with the other hand." He poured the clear fluid on the arms. Then the opposite arms. With both arms treated, he moved to their legs. With all exposed irritated skin treated, Gurefin handed the jar to a young girl and sent her back to the camp.

"Any better yet?" Gurefin asked.

"Amazing," one of the men answered.

"Your skin will be covered in a white film soon. That's normal. Leave it alone until tomorrow." Gurefin failed to inform them that the potion he shared would have left the white film from the medically active potion with or without the water.

Ponce stood in front of Juarez and produced a questioning smile. Juarez remained silent.

Manchun led the Natives off the beach. Ponce walked next to Juarez and began interrogating him about the exploration. Juarez had little to report other than he had learned that alligators usually avoided salt water. Getting no valuable news from Juarez led Ponce to ask him what he thought about the pure water.

"It worked." That is all Juarez would say about it.

"Wouldn't you like to know the source?"

"I'd rather stay out of those bushes."

"Bushes, stingrays . . . I'm sure we'll find even more uses. We're going to find the source."

"Water, water. Give me gold. Think of what you can do with gold. I've helped you accumulate gold. It made you a rich man," Juarez said.

"Yes, but it's all back in Spain. Here in Florida we're of equal wealth. That is food, water, and a place to sleep. More gold would add nothing to that. It's heavy and it sits idly in a box on the ship. The source of the water, the Fountain of Youth. Think about good health for a long time. Think about fame and the fortunes that would bring. No, the water somewhere here in Florida is the answer, much more valuable than your gold. Manchun knows the source. We need him."

"That's easy for you to say. You already have your gold. I'm here at your command, Ponce, but I would rather take some gold back to Spain and buy a villa on the coast." Juarez excused himself and settled in for a siesta.

Manchun sat with Gurefin, watching the ocean waves roll onto the beach.

"Nice job. You got them worked up to the point where they would have believed anything. Your potion in the bottom of that jar made believers out of them. Instant disciples. Not exactly blind-faith followers, but they got instant results. Misplaced belief, but then that's the way you set it up," Manchun said.

"They're gullible."

"They're in a new world, chasing after gold and now some nebulous idea of a pure-water source."

"What drives them? The idea of gold is one thing and the water mystery is intriguing. I guess it fits their religion. Blind faith. Something they want to believe, therefore, no substantive questions. How would Nonthell have said it? Perhaps, 'Are you on a solid foundation? Are your thoughts consistent with your foundation?' He was a wise man," Gurefin said.

"He was a great leader of men. He made everybody better by simply asking questions." Both men sat quietly remembering things Nonthell had taught them.

Gurefin considered what Nonthell had taught him about wealth. Nothing is more valuable than good friends, good health, and a sense of humor. The thought of material wealth bothered Gurefin. He realized that even he collected and valued polished seashells. He reconciled his discomfort by categorizing the seashells as objects of art, to be enjoyed as entities unto themselves. "You know, we collect and admire seashells for their beauty. What do you think the Spaniards do with the gold back in Spain?"

"Perhaps they use it like we do. As a medium of exchange. We trade seashells for gold, then we trade gold for conchs. In Spain, they trade gold for castles, roads, food, and horses. We've now set them up to value water," Manchun said. He leaned back on his elbows in the sand and considered the intrinsic values of gold and shells. Shells were free here on the beach. Somewhere north of his territory, gold was available for the taking. Shells here, gold there; by trading, everybody had everything they wanted.

A different view revealed that scarcity seemed to be the key. If gold were scarce in Spain, it would explain why they would come to the west for it. But what were they trading for it? What is the value to the Natives of having Spaniards in their homeland? Manchun smiled and laughed out loud. Perhaps their clumsy quests and gullibility would continue to provide some comic performances.

"Eventually, they will realize that water is free," Gurefin said.

"Ah, yes, but until then . . ."

"Until then."

CHAPTER 5

"Get my stallion ready. I'll meet you at the corrals," Ponce said. He walked to the armory, looking for Juarez. The guard told him that Juarez had been there but had left. "Find him and send him to the corrals." Ponce watched the groom cinch down his saddle and then work the horse on a lead around the corral. When the groom satisfied himself that the horse would work for Ponce, he installed the bitted bridle and led him to the waiting Ponce. Ponce pulled himself into the saddle and walked the horse quietly around the corral.

The Spaniards had brought good Spanish horses with them to the new world. The problem was that only Ponce's stallion, Rojo, and two others were properly trained. Ponce had arrived in the west knowing they had a lot of work to do before the rest of the horses would be available for battle or even dependable trail work.

Ponce and Rojo were ready for a good ride, and he ordered the gate open. "Saddle Juarez's horse and tell him to meet me on the beach." Ponce trotted his horse out. When he reached the dry sand, he walked his horse to the firm wet sand near the water's edge, then he spurred him up to a gallop.

Several Natives, including Targonsa, watched Ponce ride his big red horse. The pair appeared to be one. They changed speed, turned, stopped, backed, and raced ahead like nothing Targonsa had ever seen. Targonsa didn't recognize anything clumsy or out of place about the Spaniard he had been critical of. With his horse, Ponce was to be respected, even feared. This show put a different perspective on the Natives' situation.

Soon Juarez, riding a heavier black horse with a long mane and tail, raced to join Ponce on the wet sand. The men and horses moved in concert as if they were in a well-choreographed dance routine. Targonsa watched, mesmerized and totally consumed in the transformation of the clumsy Spaniards. In his flowered paradise, Targonsa had never wanted for anything. He never lusted after anything the Spaniards had or talked about. Now that changed. He wanted to ride a horse.

Ponce asked Juarez as they walked the horses down the sandy beach, "How many horses do we have that are fully trained?"

"These two and one more. Farming and construction have slowed training too much. I've got the saddles and gear stored in a secure log building. I've only got two men that know how to train horses and do it right."

"Get them working all day every day. We brought three stallions and twenty-two mares. One mare died on the ship, I can understand that, but one died last week. Why?"

"She colicked. The feed here is a problem. The salt grasses aren't right for them. But seven of the mares were pregnant and now we've got seven foals in the herd."

"Good. What are you going to do about feed?"

"It's too risky to drive the herd over the hills to an inland meadow. We'll have to make hay over there and bring it back with the horses loaded."

"Let's get with it. We're going to need these horses."

The next day, Juarez took three men over the nearby hills to the meadow and had them cut the tall grasses. Over the next few days, they tended and raked the grass into bundles as it dried, tied up the bundles, and carried them home on pack horses. The herd responded well to their new feed. Juarez assigned the three men to continue the haying operations until the barn next to the saddle and tack building was full. Meanwhile, the two trainers went to work on the raw horses.

Targonsa found a hillside vantage from which he could watch the men work with the horses. He studied everything they did. How they worked the horses until they could tie a lead rope on their heads. How they taught the horses to respect the men and the ropes. He watched how large motions were used to get horses to do little things, then he studied how the horses learned to do more with smaller motions from the men. What impressed Targonsa more than anything was how the horses learned to respond to the most minute cues. He began to see how Ponce and Juarez could ride and make it look effortless.

Targonsa went to Manchun and told him he wanted to talk to the Spaniards about the horses. Manchun told him to try. Targonsa went to the settlement alone and asked about the horses. The guard sent him with another guard to find Juarez.

"I would like to watch the men work with the horses," Targonsa said.

"Maybe you'd like to help," Juarez replied.

"I can learn."

"Good. Follow me." Juarez led Targonsa to the corral and introduced him to the trainers.

"This man wants to help with the horses. Maybe he can help by cleaning the pens," Juarez said.

"There's a lot of work here. We'll show him what to do," one of the men said.

Targonsa couldn't believe it was going to be this easy to be around the horses. He would do almost anything to be close to the horses.

"Watch us from outside the fence for a while, then we'll give you something to do."

Targonsa again admired the work as he watched the men start with big motions that reduced to small and almost imperceptible movements while the horses learned to do more with less.

Juarez had hand-picked these trainers. They rejected brutal training methods most others used to work with horses. Juarez could be brutal with men and impatient with circumstances, especially when gold was at stake. But when horses were in the equation, Juarez adopted a different attitude. The trainers demonstrated that attitude in everything they did.

One of the men asked Targonsa if he wanted to come in and walk a horse around the pen. Targonsa accepted the end of the rope. His job was to walk and keep the horse behind him and slightly off his right shoulder. Targonsa had watched the men do this and it looked simple. Doing it for the first time was different. The horse didn't stay behind him or to his right. The man showed Targonsa how to make it easy for the horse to do the right thing and hard to do the wrong thing. When the horse tried to move ahead, a small jerk back corrected the error. When the horse tried to move behind him, shortening the rope and putting pressure on the head moved the horse into position.

Targonsa learned quickly and soon had the horse under control and moving in concert with him. The two men were impressed. By the end of the day, they thought they finally had some much-needed help. Then the Spaniards gave Targonsa another job—to clean the horse manure from the pens. Targonsa asked if he could come back to help with the horses. The men said yes. "Tell the guard and he will bring you to us."

Targonsa came back and looked forward to many days with the horses. Horse trainers are special people. The horse is everything. Good trainers are not mean, or greedy, or in a hurry. The Spanish trainers recognized those traits in Targonsa. They increasingly gave him new training routines and responsibilities. They ordered two new small circle pens to be built so that each of the three men could work with horses independently. Targonsa gladly continued to clean the pens as well.

Before long, the Spanish trainers had a few horses ready for bareback riders. They called Targonsa to a pen with one horse and explained what they intended to do, how they would prepare the horse, and what they would do from the horse's back. The groundwork the trainers had accomplished now proved invaluable. The horse stood quietly and confidently. The trainer led the horse to the fence, stepped up onto the fence, then gently positioned a leg over the horse's back. Slowly he shifted his weight onto the horse. The horse stood quietly. As the rider had explained to Targonsa, he used his heels and thighs to communicate with the horse. The lead rope on the horse's head gave the rider control. Targonsa watched and hoped he would get a chance. The rider made it easy for the horse to do the right things. He made no big corrections and didn't ask for any difficult footwork.

After a few minutes, the rider stopped the horse and slowly slid off her back. He asked Targonsa if he wanted to try it. Targonsa moved quickly into the pen and took the lead rope. He had watched carefully. He replicated every step the trainer had taken. When he shifted his weight onto the horse, he felt an exhilaration like nothing he had ever experienced. He squeezed his legs around the horse and the horse walked out. The Spaniards were impressed. Learning and training as usual continued for days.

The training routine now shifted. Each of the three trainers would select a horse and be responsible for the training. The Spanish trainers told Targonsa they would watch him and correct him if necessary. They also encouraged him to ask when he had any questions. Targonsa selected a horse and led his assignment out of the large holding pen to his small circle pen. The young reddish-brown mare followed him without incident.

Two days later, Targonsa asked the Spanish trainers to come to his pen and watch him take his first bareback ride. They finished what they had in hand and walked to Targonsa and his young mare. Targonsa proceeded as he'd learned when he'd ridden the first time. The mare stood quietly while Targonsa took his seat. He squeezed his heels and the mare moved forward. Targonsa stopped her, turned her and reversed directions. Then he put his heels in her with more force than when he started. The mare responded. She jumped forward into an instant gallop. Targonsa went off her back and landed flat in the dirt. The mare stopped cold without her rider. Targonsa jumped up and walked slowly to the horse. He picked up the lead rope and led her to his friends.

"What happened?" Targonsa asked.

"She did exactly what you told her to do. You applied more pressure than she was expecting for a walk. She's very sensitive. She's going to be a good horse. Are you okay?"

"I'm embarrassed."

"We've all done it. It happens. Now you know how much pressure to apply. The day will come when you'll want her to jump out like that. You'll be ready for it, and you'll be happy. One more thing you must do. Get back on her to convince her that you're okay with her. You don't want to teach her that she can lose a rider and get away with it. Okay?"

"Yes. Sure." Targonsa led the mare to the fence and got back on. He squeezed gently and she walked out. A few trips around the pen and the Spanish trainer gave Targonsa permission to get off and give the young mare some friendly rubs. They told Targonsa they liked to ride the horses bareback before they put the saddles on them; soon they would take the new horses to the beach. That sounded good. In two days Targonsa learned to ride at a trot and at a gallop. Three horses were ready to ride out to the beach.

Good things grew from the horse training. Ponce approved of the horse-training regimen. Juarez needed horses to lead the conquest of gold-sourcing Natives. The Spanish hay-packing crew had stuffed the small shed tightly with hay all the way to the roof. Other than Targonsa, the Natives had little contact with the Spaniards. All was good—until Targonsa started down the beach to meet his horse-training friends and noticed a trail of smoke rising from the Spanish compound.

When he reached the gates, he was told to hurry to the horses. As he reached them, the two Spanish trainers were trying to control the horses. Targonsa joined the trainers without a second thought. The men, with calm voices and slow movements, comforted the horses, but that was the only good news. The hay shed and adjoining tack room, with all the saddles, had burned to the ground. No food for the horses and no equipment for the next phase of training depressed everybody.

Ponce stood at the scene and shouted at everybody. Then he asked the trainers what they were going to do. One trainer said they had to feed the horses. Ponce wanted to know how they were going to do that. The trainer said they would have to cut some of the local low-quality grass nearby. Ponce told them to do it. He thought about that for a moment, then asked about the next day and after that. The trainer said they would have to bring some more hay in from the distant meadows.

The second trainer walked to Ponce. "How about we build a fence at the meadow and move the horses out there? We could set up a small camp there and continue training."

"How long would it take to build that fence?"

"That depends on how many men you put on it."

"I'll send twenty men with you today. You show them exactly what you need."

"Okay."

Ponce organized twenty workers, a cook, supplies, and equipment. He told the men to stay until they finished the fence. The two Spanish horse trainers thought that was the best news they had received since they reached the new world. Targonsa went home and the workers trudged off toward the meadows.

A week later, one of the horse trainers walked up the beach toward the trail to Manchun's camp. He met a young boy and asked for Targonsa. The boy said he would run and get him. The Spaniard told Targonsa that they had finished the fence at the meadow, and they had to move the horses. They didn't have enough riders that could ride bareback to move the herd. He asked if Targonsa would help. Targonsa replied that he wanted to help.

In the morning, Targonsa met the trainers at the horse pen; they were holding the lead ropes on the new horses they had trained. A trainer gave Targonsa a headstall and told him to catch his red mare. Targonsa entered the pen and moved slowly to the horse he had trained. He put the headgear on her and walked her to the gate. As he walked the horse in small circles to prepare her for a ride, Ponce, Juarez, and a third rider showed up. They entered the pen and came out with their personal well-trained horses.

Ponce, Juarez, and the third man were excellent riders and showed confidence being on the horses bareback. The trainers made the point that most of the horses had rarely or never been out of the pen and that they might be hard to control. One trainer opened the gate and the other trainer rode into the pen to push the horses out. The horses exited the pen and trotted into low-quality grass to eat. The riders formed a line behind them and moved forward together. The herd continued to nibble grass as they moved away from the riders.

The six riders pushed the herd toward the hills and the meadows beyond. Targonsa watched the other riders work with the herd. He studied how they positioned themselves, the distance between them and the herd, and how quickly they moved to keep a stray horse from breaking ranks. For two hours, the herd moved compliantly as they nibbled the grass and moved on ahead of the riders. The trail left the moist soil and followed higher terrain that was rougher and drier. The herd lost their concentration on eating. As the space the herd occupied increased, the riders intensified their efforts. They moved up closer to the herd on the left and right, attempting to keep them together.

The horses had survived confinement in a ship, had survived confinement in an inadequate pen, and had even survived second-rate feed. Now, after snacking freely on fresh grass, they were being pushed away from the grass they wanted. A stallion activated the herd. He pushed four mares to the front of the pack and broke them away from the rest. He circled and exerted his dominance over the mares about twenty yards from the rest of the horses. Ponce and one of the trainers rode quickly to contain the small group and get them back into line. The stallion had his own agenda, though, and pushed his harem off toward the hills at a gallop. Ponce and the trainer rode after them.

That activity broke the herd continuity. The horses scattered in a matter of seconds. Small groups of horses ran off in different directions. Two groups of horses with foals moved off to the right. Juarez, the second trainer, and the third rider went off after them. That left Targonsa to chase down the remaining horses that galloped off to the left into trees and brush. Targonsa squeezed his legs and anticipated the surge of power from his red mare. It came and he was one with his horse. They raced into the trees. Once in the trees, Targonsa slowed the ride to a walk and followed the hoofprints. He listened for the hard beats of galloping horses. He couldn't hear anything. He assumed they were walking somewhere ahead of him. He followed the hoofprints through the forested area until the trees thinned where small patches of grass and pools of water emerged.

He inspected the ground around one of the pools. The horses had stopped here. Hoofprints had churned the ground, and they had walked to the edge of the water to drink. Targonsa moved his horse to the water for a drink, then they continued the hunt. After an hour, Targonsa caught a glimpse of one horse and assumed she wasn't alone. His priority should be to stop them from moving away from the hills they had to cross. Targonsa set a course he hoped would allow him to circle the small group, and then he could try to push them toward the hills. His ideas proved effective. He managed to position himself on the far side of the horses. Now he hoped he could make it easy for them to do the right thing.

Within sight of the horses, he held his position and let the horses watch him as he watched them. When they all looked comfortable, he moved forward. The small herd held their position. Slow and steady seemed like a strategy that might work. Finally, the horses moved toward the hills. Targonsa kept the herd between him and where he wanted them to go. Every time a horse drifted out of line, Targonsa slowed and then circled around them to consolidate the herd. Only twice did Targonsa find it necessary to gallop to redirect the stray herd. Early in the evening, Targonsa pushed the herd near the summit of the hills. He noticed hoofprints that indicated that many horses had been over the trail. He continued to push his small herd.

At the fenced pasture in the meadow, the Spaniards had started a fire but had nothing to eat.

"We lost that stallion and all four mares from my group," Ponce said.

"We lost one mare and her foal. I suppose we lost all the horses that Indian chased," Juarez said.

"I think he'll show up. He's really good with horses," one of the trainers said.

Targonsa pushed on. The sun dropped below a cloud bank on the coast when he spotted the fire at the meadow. He continued. Just before dark, the moon began to rise over the horizon. Targonsa moved the horses near the fence before the Spaniards noticed he had all five of the horses he had chased. They opened the gate and helped move them into the pasture.

"Good job," one of the trainers said.

"Come in by the fire. Have some water. We don't have anything to eat," Ponce said.

"Listen," said Targonsa. "Hear that? We can have frog legs if you'll help me catch them." The Spaniards jumped at that. They slept on the sandy ground with full bellies.

In the morning, they caught the riding horses, inspected the fence, and rode back to the settlement. Ponce agreed to build a shelter at the meadow and have the trainers stay there to complete the training. Even without saddles, they were going to need the horses. They didn't think to invite Targonsa to stay at the meadows. The Spaniards built a skimpy shelter and arranged to deliver supplies as needed. The trainers weren't disappointed to be away from the settlement. They were horse people.

Six days later, as Targonsa roamed the hills north of the meadows hunting for a deer, he saw a horse running free. He climbed to a high point and tried to determine why the horse was free. The horse disappeared, and Targonsa couldn't see any other activity. The next day, he walked on the beach and decided to tell the Spaniards about the horse. He walked to the compound and asked about the trainers. The guard said they were dead. Targonsa asked about the horses. The guard said they were gone. He decided to talk to Ponce about his friends and the horses. The guard sent for Ponce.

"No need to come here. No more horses," Ponce said even before he reached a respectable speaking distance.

"What happened?"

"A bear broke into the pasture. The trainers tried to save the horses, but the bear killed the men. The horses all escaped, except one of the foals."

Targonsa thought about it. "I can catch your horses."

"How are you going to do that?"

"I can run, and you know I can ride and herd the horses. If you give me a headstall, I can do it."

"Then you go get our horses."

"I will want something for it."

"What?"

"If I bring you four horses, I want that red horse I trained."

"No."

"Okay." Targonsa turned to leave.

Ponce thought about that. If he didn't accept Targonsa's offer, Targonsa would probably try to catch the horses regardless. "Okay, but five horses."

Targonsa continued to walk.

"Alright. Four horses. Follow me, I'll get you a headstall."

At first light, Targonsa trotted off with his medicine bag, his bow and arrows, and the headstall toward the hills where he'd seen the loose horse. A full day and he only found the hoofprints of a single horse. The tracks, although not fresh, consistently pointed north. He decided to follow them the next day. By midday, he discovered good news. The trail he followed merged with two more horses' prints. Just before dark, he caught sight of the three horses.

Targonsa thought out his best option. He could move closer in the dead of night, or he could stay put and start again in the morning. He knew he wanted to keep them calm and decided not to take a chance of spooking them in the dark. In the daylight, the horses were gone again. He trotted to the spot where he had seen them and continued to follow the tracks. Midmorning, an exceptional vantage point on a hill overlooked the convergence of two meadows separated by the hill he stood upon. He couldn't believe his good luck. The three horses he had been following grazed in the small meadow on the right. Four more stood in the meadow to his left. His smile brightened when he recognized one of the four was his red mare. That mare, he thought, would be the most likely to accept him in the area.

He set a course off the hill that kept him out of sight and quiet. When he reached the meadow, the horses were grazing peacefully. He knew he had to reveal himself and hope his mare didn't run off with the other horses. He stood tall in the grasses and moved slowly. When the horses noticed him, they moved away, keeping their distance. Targonsa slowed his pace. His red mare directed her attention to him. He extended his hand with the palm up and moved forward, a small step at a time.

The other three horses walked away. The red mare started off with them but stopped. Targonsa thought about that. No other animal he had ever seen wanted to be with humans. Horses were different. Targonsa stopped and let her think about it. He continued the game for over an hour before the red mare allowed him to approach within touching distance. Rather than risk losing the trust he had established, Targonsa allowed the mare to reach out to him. He stood still with his hand extended. The mare finally touched his hand with her nose. He remained frozen, until she applied pressure on his hand. Then, he moved his fingers under her chin and scratched her lightly. She accepted that, so he placed his hand on her neck and rubbed her gently. Before he attempted to put the headstall on her, he rubbed her back and neck. Finally, he attached the headstall, walked her around the meadow, and jumped up onto her back.

Once on horseback, he walked the mare around the other horses to put them at ease. It didn't take long before he could move those three horses around the hill to meet up with the other three that he had followed to this area. Six free horses and the red mare started back toward home.

The two-day trip home proved uneventful. As Targonsa neared his camp, he contemplated the disposition of the six horses. He agreed to return four horses. Should he give Ponce the extra two horses? Could he negotiate for the two horses? Maybe he would keep them and train them for his friends. He decided to leave two horses with friends away from his camp and well away from the Spaniards for the time being. He wanted to test Ponce's honor.

Targonsa stopped his herd at a remote site with friends. He showed them how to build a makeshift pen and gave them instructions for feed and care. The next day, they drove two horses into the pen and Targonsa continued toward the beach, riding the red mare and driving the four horses for the Spaniards. The Spaniards noticed him on the beach and called for Ponce. A contingent of men from the settlement with ropes moved toward the herd. They surrounded the herd and managed to get ropes on the four horses.

Ponce approached Targonsa. "You did a good job."

"We had a time, but I found them."

"I want the red horse as well. I'll give you something else."

That was the response Targonsa feared and, in some ways, expected. "That's not the deal we made."

"I'll give you something else."

"What would I want more than this red mare?"

"How about some food from our gardens?"

Targonsa laughed, then said, "Food? I've got all the food I need." He spread his arms to show that his food sources encompassed everything from the ocean to the forests and swamps.

"How about a knife?"

"How about you living up to your word?"

Ponce stood in silence. Once again, he had been put in his place by what he considered an uneducated and uncivilized Indian.

Targonsa sat quietly on the mare to let Ponce stew on his dilemma. Ponce watched his men lead the horses back to the settlement.

"If I let you keep the mare—"

Targonsa cut him off, "You mean if you keep your word."

"Yes, yes. With the mare, could you catch more of the horses?"

"Don't know. What would you give for each horse?"

"How about a knife for each horse?"

"How about a knife and a long sword for each horse?"

"I'll give you a knife for each horse and a machete for two horses."

"I'll see what I can do, but the mare is mine."

"Okay." Ponce trudged back to the settlement and his four horses.

Targonsa made regular trips to his friends with the horses and taught them how to train and ride.

CHAPTER 6

Manchun queried Targonsa about his experience with the Spaniards. Targonsa told him the only Spaniards he trusted were the horse trainers, and they were dead. Manchun shook his head when he heard about Ponce trying to renege on his deal. He told Targonsa he didn't want the Spaniards to have any more horses. He said he thought they should make every effort to drive any free horses as far north as possible and that he was happy that their friends with the horses were learning to ride.

"Ponce is not fit, and I think he's just plain tired of fighting. He's gullible and he doesn't have much of a moral foundation. I think he's being pushed by that Juarez character. I think if Ponce could find the source of the water, he'd be perfectly happy. But watch out for Juarez. He's got an agenda," Manchun said.

"The source of the water is rain. What's wrong with him?" Gurefin said and then laughed about the mystery of the water.

"You've got him hooked on something magical about it. What else can we do to keep him on the string?" Targonsa said.

"I don't know, but we should never miss an opportunity," Manchun said.

The weather changed, trees bent to the wind, and everybody retreated to shelter for two days. Even through a windy and rainy morning, a guard recognized the vessel flying the Spanish flag anchored near their own ship. The alarm went out and Ponce with Juarez ordered the longboat launched with four oarsmen. The wind whipped the bay waters into whitecaps with blowing water and rain that soon accumulated in the boat to create a sloshing wash around the Spaniards' boots. The oarsmen worked, and Ponce directed the boat to the newly arrived ship.

The look of the supply ship foretold her mission. She would never be confused with a pleasure craft nor a well-maintained and disciplined warship. The worn and tired craft reeked of animal waste. Less-than-efficient sailors tried to obey orders from the captain, and other officers shouted from a pulpit above the soiled deck. The captain asked Ponce if he wanted to come aboard. Ponce focused on the waste flowing overboard and declined.

The captain called for a sailor to deliver the manifest to Ponce. Rice, wheat, gunpowder, and lead. Animals included pigs: a boar, a pregnant sow, and ten young pigs. As welcome as the pigs were the crates of chickens. Twenty chickens and a rooster came over the gunwale first. Ponce's men stacked the wet hens in the bow. A crate with the boar and the sow landed in the longboat's sloshing water. The grains and munitions packed in watertight chests came next. Before the loose young pigs were lowered, the captain called to Ponce and told him he was delivering a new libation rather than wine. He said they called it rum and that it was made here in the new world. That news disappointed Ponce, but he would take what he could get.

After the cases of rum landed in the longboat, she sat low in the water. The captain ordered his men to begin lowering the young pigs one at a time. Each of the loose squealing pigs in the longboat caused more frustration for the oarsmen. When the last pig entered the longboat, Ponce called up to the captain and told him they needed more horses and twenty saddles. The captain waved and bid Ponce farewell. The pigs disrupted the oarsmen's ability to row efficiently. The sailors cursed the pigs as they fought for rowing positions and against blowing seawater.

Eighteen wet Spaniards waited on the beach to help land the longboat and transport contents back to the compound. The oarsmen kicked pigs out of their way as they tried to obey Ponce's orders to align the boat to the beach. When he thought he had it about right, Ponce gave the order for the final push onto the beach. Unfortunately for the boat, simultaneous to the order came a rogue quartering wave that turned the longboat and sent it parallel with the next wave. The overloaded craft succumbed to gravity and capsized. All passengers and contents went adrift into the surging surf.

All the Spaniards jumped to and ran to rescue everything they could get their hands on. The two watertight chests were afloat, and Ponce ordered two men to get them to the beach. Two of the three chicken crates broke open and wet hens and the rooster were free on the beach. The crate that held the boar and sow no longer existed. The boar and sow were last seen running from the beach. Ten young pigs squealed and teased the Spaniards as they tried to catch them. Ponce pulled himself from the sea and gave the captain from the supply ship a one-armed demeaning salute as the ship raised the anchor and moved away under sail. Juarez waded to the case containing the rum and dragged it to shore.

Gurefin, Petnima, and a few other Natives watched the melee on the beach. They noticed the boar and sow disappear and wondered about their disposition. The wet hens loose on the sand fluttered about and cried out, adding to the confusion. The squealing pigs being ineffectually chased made the Natives laugh. They watched the rooster flutter off the sand into the protective bushes, while Ponce and Juarez worked to pull the longboat onto the beach.

"There'll be no wine or rest until all ten pigs and these chickens are safe in the compound," Ponce shouted.

Juarez reached down and caught a chicken in both hands. "Take this one to the compound and get back out here," he shouted.

"Where do I put this one?" a Spaniard shouted as he held a pig against his chest with both hands.

"Put him in the compound pen, then get back here," Ponce shouted back.

When the chickens were caught, all hands concentrated on the pigs. The young pigs wanted to be together, but they didn't want to be caught. Twelve Spaniards surrounded the pigs and tried to keep them encircled. The Spaniards tried to rush the pigs. The pigs avoided capture and ran to the bushes. Now off the sand and into more fertile soil, the pigs wallowed in mud. A Spaniard moved toward a pig with caution. When he thought he could catch him, he lunged. The pig lurched and the Spaniard landed face first in the mud. Three men surrounded a pig and reached out to put a hand on him. The pig squirmed free and as one of the men sprang after him, he landed flat in the mud on his back. The hilarious spat in the mud continued until midday, when the final pig made his last stand and the Spaniards retreated to their compound.

With the longboat stowed, all chests and cases retrieved, and the last pig captured, Ponce ordered the gates closed. Ponce and Juarez inspected the chicken pen and the pig pen. Then they went to a dry room to assure that the sealed chests had survived the crash landing. The rice, wheat, munitions, and miscellaneous supplies had survived. Ponce told Juarez they should bathe and then try some of the rum they had acquired. Juarez agreed.

Ponce ordered up a big fire and hot water for a bath. He soaked and contemplated the supply-ship experience. Additional supplies and livestock would depend on Ponce ordering his sailing ship back to Hispaniola. As governor, Ponce determined the supply-ship captain would be punished. He would talk to Juarez about it. Ponce dressed, sat in front of the fire, and waited for Juarez.

"Have you tried the rum yet?" Juarez asked.

"I was waiting for you." Ponce went to the crate, broke it open clumsily, and retrieved a bottle and two cups. With no experience with rum, they assumed a potency like wine. Ponce poured a cup for each of them and joined Juarez in front of the fire.

"That warms things up all the way down," Juarez said.

"Not bad. That was a mess on the beach. Aside from the boar and the sow, what did we lose?"

"There was one dead chicken, and the rooster is missing."

"If he doesn't show up, we'll miss him. Any chance we'll ever see the boar and sow again?"

"I doubt it. They were making fast tracks off the beach. I'm going to miss those roast pigs."

Ponce gulped another mouthful of rum. "Ah that's pretty good. The only decent thing I can say about that captain.

"I don't want to take the time to sail back to Hispaniola, but I guess we could do it. In any event, I'm going to continue sending short exploratory trips out to learn more about what we've got."

"It's either that, or we learn to eat what's here. I don't want to miss my chicken and roast pig." Juarez joined Ponce in tipping the cups up again. "We should get more of this rum, too." They continued to soak up the warmth from the fire.

After a period of silence, Ponce went to the bottle of rum and refilled both cups. He returned to his chair and flopped down uncere-moniously. "I want to go north."

In a slurred speech, Juarez agreed and said, "Sooo dooo I."

Ponce's speech was now equally impaired. "I want that water source. Think how great that would be."

"Not as good as this. I want the source of the nuggets."

"We can get both, all of it. We can have it all."

They finished their second cup and went for yet another and began talking about visions of grandiosity, women, wealth, and fame.

"Think how famous we'll be when we find the Fountain of Youth."

"I've got a girlfriend in Hispaniola that will marry me if I bring back gold."

"We'll get some gold too."

"No, you don't know Francesca. She likes a lot of gold. I should have joined up with Pizarro or Cortés."

"I don't think so. You wouldn't have gotten a percentage. You would be sleeping on the ground and eating outside with the rest of the foot soldiers."

"Maybe you're right."

They finished the bottle and shortly passed out in front of the fire. A grand hangover greeted them in the morning. They suffered all day and avoided all interactions.

The wind quit and the sun shone upon Gurefin and his son. "Well son, what would you have done differently from the way the Spaniards landed on the beach yesterday?"

"Gee Dad, that's a hard one."

"Try."

"Maybe wait a day. Then, unload on a sunny day with no wind. Maybe like today. Or maybe make two or three trips. Maybe bring a line from the ship to the shore and slide the stuff down the rope. Maybe, if the ship had to leave, they could have moved it all onto the other ship. Maybe they could learn to live without any of it."

Gurefin and his son smiled broadly at the Spaniards' errors. "Can you summarize it in one word?"

The boy cocked his head and said flatly, "Stupid."

"Yeah, now can you do it with a smart word?"

"Patience?"

"That'll do. It sounded like they called those new animals 'pigs.' Those big ones that ran off could be dangerous. Be careful if you see them."

"They called those birds 'chickens' and they really wanted that big pretty one."

"That must have been the male."

"How can I catch him?"

"You heard him this morning, didn't you?"

"Yeah."

"Don't let the Spaniards know what you're up to. I would start by listening for him. Then watch him. When you know what he likes to eat, where he sleeps, and how he spends his days, you'll be ready to build a trap."

"I'm going to catch him."

"The Spaniards will want to trade something for him. Let me help with that."

That ended formal school for the day. Gurefin's son went out to the lab to ply what he'd learned.

Juarez went to Ponce and said, "If we have to be here, let's enjoy it and roast a pig."

"We'll need a big firepit. I don't want another fire in here. Let's do it on the beach."

That was all Juarez needed. He left quickly and issued orders to make it happen. Juarez directed a pit to be dug just off the sandy beach and the collection of palm leaves and enough firewood to develop a deep bed of coals. The Natives watched and wondered what the Spaniards would do with such a huge fire. Manchun walked down the beach to find out. They told him that the next day, when the coals were right, they would roast one of the pigs and have a fiesta. Manchun returned to his camp and asked two young people to keep their distance while they watched and learned.

The Spaniards lined the pit with rocks and built their fire. They collected more wood, rocks, and palm fronds, just as they had done on Hispaniola. The next morning, the Spaniards wrapped the butchered pig in palm leaves and placed the package on the rocks covering the coals. Then they placed more rocks on and around the bundle, then more leaves and rocks to hold it all in place. They left it alone and only occasionally returned to check on it. Nothing appeared to change, and they apparently thought that was good. Late in the afternoon, a group returned to the cooking operation with a large rack, knives, and gloves. They removed the rocks and cut and peeled the leaves away. With great care, they revealed the cooked pig. The aroma wafted across the beach and impressed the Natives. The Spaniards, almost ceremoniously, worked to place the pig on the rack and carry it into the compound.

The fiesta was on. Music and laughter emanated from the compound as they picked away at their coveted delicacy. The Natives, based on the fragrance from the pit, agreed that it must be something to be celebrated. Until the cooking of the pig, horses were the only thing the Spaniards brought that the Natives had wanted. They now had horses but thought that a pig might be worth working for. Perhaps the boar and the sow would produce some pigs they could capture.

Gurefin's son continued his quest for the rooster. He had spent two days watching how the bird spent his days and nights. He thought he might be able to capture him with a box trap baited with grain heads and lush leaves. He built a lightweight cage with small sticks and placed it amongst the bushes. He propped up one end with a stick that he tied a string to. He stretched the string to his concealed hiding place.

He waited. While he waited, he thought about his discussion with his father regarding the Spaniards' impatience, demonstrated when they transported the rooster onto the beach. With the virtue of patience, he waited. Hours later, the rooster entered one of his favorite clearings. He pecked and scratched. As he neared the trap, Gurefin's son held his breath. His plans and patience were about to be rewarded. Finally, he pulled the string. The trap fell. The rooster screeched. He had his rooster.

Back at the glen by the river, Gurefin helped build a larger holding pen and congratulated his son. "What are you going to do with him?"

"I don't know. I don't think we should eat him."

"No, I don't either. Shall we trade him to the Spaniards? I'm sure they want him."

"Do you think we could get a horse?"

"Probably not."

"A pig?"

"Probably not."

"Maybe we'll have to settle for some conchs."

"Let's start with a horse and go from there."

"Okay."

Gurefin went to the Spanish settlement and asked to have a talk with Ponce. Ponce came to the gate where Gurefin waited. "How are your chickens?" Gurefin asked.

"They're laying eggs for us."

"No babies, I guess."

"Not without a rooster."

"What's the rooster worth to you?"

"Do you have our rooster?"

"No, we have our rooster."

"There's only one rooster and it's ours."

"Where do you keep it?"

Ponce scratched his head and had a confounded look on his face. "It's loose out there somewhere. You know that."

"Well, we have a rooster that's not loose."

"That's mine."

"No, it's ours. Maybe we'll trade it."

Ponce abandoned his line of argument and fell into Gurefin's premise. Now the rooster was trade bait. The only question that remained would revolve around—trade for what? Ponce looked back into the friendliness of his compound. Everything outside that fence created a sense of vulnerability. "Okay, what do you want for it?"

"We'll take one of the horses."

"No. I can't do that. The horses are under Juarez's control and he will never give up another one."

"That's too bad. Maybe we'll eat the rooster."

"You shouldn't do that," Ponce quickly said with a worried look.

Gurefin shifted his weight and tightened his lips. He waited several seconds before he replied, "Maybe two pigs would be okay. I have to please other people as well."

Ponce reflected on his importance as governor of all the land he stood upon and decided to play the part. "No. One pig is all I will give you for the rooster."

"Are you a man of your word?"

That question knocked Ponce off his pompous attitude, since his word had been questioned before. "Of course I am."

"Okay. We'll meet you on the beach. Bring the pig and we'll give you the rooster."

"Alright," Ponce said as he sighed in relief that the negotiations ended.

Gurefin, Gurefin's son, and Manchun brought the rooster to the beach and exchanged it for a pig. They would have a fiesta of their own.

CHAPTER 7

Juarez took control of the horses and their training, and he convinced Ponce to allow him to expand exploratory missions. The first question at all the debriefings hinged on gold. Did they find any gold? Did they see rocks or black sand that could contain gold? Did they see any landscapes that resembled Puerto Rico where they did find gold? The answers were always no.

"Nothing, you found nothing of any value?"

"We found long stretches of open grasslands and we caught a glimpse of one horse."

"One of our loose horses?"

"Had to be one of ours. We found the tracks and tried to catch up to it, but we lost the trail in a huge swampy area."

"Why would a horse leave grassland for a swamp?"

"It wasn't a swamp; more like a huge wet meadow."

"I want you to go back up there and have a good look around. Take enough supplies for a week if necessary. If we can find where the horses are settled, we'll go get them." Juarez picked two more men to accompany the men that had just returned. The five men marched out of the settlement two days later.

The trek over the low-lying coastal hills proved uneventful and the men relished being out of the compound. When they reached the grasslands, they spread out, looking for signs of the horses. Finding none, their enthusiasm was dampened. By the time they reached the wet marshy area north of the grasslands, finding only a few old horse droppings told them the horses had moved on. Just before sunset, one man watched a horse and rider on a low hill to the west. He reported the sighting, and the group contemplated the next day's quest from around the campfire. They decided to move up through the marshy area while they kept the line of western hills in sight.

The marshlands' wet ground, small pools of water, rotting fallen trees, and uncertain trails slowed their progress. Trekking no longer intrigued them; moving through this area required work and concentration. They hoped they would get through it and rejoin more grasslands soon. If they didn't, they would move over to the hills to have a look around.

Two men, on their last trip, thought the horses had moved into this area, but now there was no sign of them. The heat made the fourth afternoon miserable. They stopped for a break and decided to leave the marshes and climb onto the hills as soon as possible. One of them flung his pack onto a fallen tree trunk, then sat on the ground and leaned back against the trunk. When he leaned back, he knocked the pack off the tree to the ground on the other side. The other four men found places to rest and cool off, too. After a twenty-minute break, the man leaning against the tree kneeled, leaned over the tree trunk, and groped for his pack without paying attention.

"Ow!" he yelled. He pulled back and raised his arm with a snake still clinging to his wrist. He stood and tried to pull the snake away from his wrist. Finally, he freed himself from the snake and killed it. He crumpled to the ground and appeared to be in severe shock with a lot of pain. The men gathered around him and tried to console him while they asked what he was feeling. Meanwhile, they moved the dead black, yellow, and red snake aside. The man said there was pain in his wrist and that he needed to rest some more. He didn't think he could walk. For an hour, the men waited, watched, and contemplated plans to get the victim out of the marshlands. During that time, the man's speech became slurred and he reported that his vision was failing. At the end of the hour, he was dead.

That incident changed plans dramatically. That lethal snake was new to them. They had to report it, but they also had to get their dead companion back to the settlement for a religious burial. Now, getting away from the marshlands seemed the most critical concern. They cautiously put the snake in a bag. One man collected the pack and the largest and strongest man lifted the victim onto his shoulder, and they started toward the low hills. Two hours of nonstop trudging through muck and wet grasses rewarded them with dry ground at the foot of the small hills.

A quick camp setup and a search for suitable limbs to build a transport to carry the victim occupied the tired men before they tried to eat with minimal light. With nothing to do in the dark, the men's minds went numb, remembering their friend's last moments. Sleep avoided the men, and they rose at first light, weary of thoughts about what lurked unseen in this new world. Alligators and snakes were unpleasant and deadly, but what they didn't know now concerned them. The thought of the soothing and life-saving pure water Ponce sought failed to console them.

Their overriding concern for returning the dead man to the settlement for a funeral forced them to push their endurance. They neglected the stallion pile near the trail and even the two Natives on horseback watching them from high on the hilltops. They completed the trip home in less than two days. A guard noticed them approaching on the beach and sounded the alarm. Ponce and two escorts met the expedition on the beach. Gurefin and Petnima noticed the activity and joined them.

Ponce asked what happened to his soldier. They told him it was a snake bite. He asked if it was a rattlesnake. They told him no and emptied the sack holding the dead snake. Petnima jumped back.

"Too bad you didn't have any pure water; sometimes it can draw out the poison from a three-colored-snake bite," Gurefin said, knowing that it was unlikely they would encounter another snake like it.

"We've got to get to the source," Ponce said.

Gurefin looked him in the eyes. It was the first time Ponce had made direct reference to getting the water for himself. "That would be our water in a special place."

"I think we need some for ourselves. For things like bites from three-colored snakes."

"We rarely need it for snake bites."

"Why's that?" Ponce said in a demanding voice.

"Because we share the land with them. We don't bother them; they don't bother us."

"They bother us."

"Maybe you should learn to share."

"We don't want to share with the snakes. No, we're not going to share."

"Maybe we won't share any more pure water."

"I didn't say anything about you. We share with you. Oh yes, we're a very sharing people."

That seemed like a strange statement coming from the Spaniard, Petnima thought. Since they arrived, their only activity had been to isolate themselves behind the walls of their settlement. Where is my ...? Where can I get more? What will you give me for ...? "What have you shared with us?"

Ponce looked toward Petnima, a bit shocked that a woman would question him. He looked back to Gurefin. "We shared the conchs with you."

"No, you didn't. You traded them for our gold. And you took them from our fishery."

Ponce didn't respond. Instead, he directed his men to bring the body into the settlement. The Spaniards left the beach. Gurefin and Petnima watched them disappear beyond the settlement gate.

"I don't trust them," Petnima said. She rolled her eyes and shook her head slightly. "Manchun has warned us about them. Let them go share their ignorance."

Ponce and Juarez held a briefing with the remaining expedition force. They noted the circumstances of the snake bite. They took great interest when the men told them they spotted two bareback riders on the hills.

"Two. We only gave them one." Ponce stopped speaking and contemplated his own statement. In his most secret thoughts, he knew he hadn't given them anything. "Was one of the horses my stallion?"

"No, one of the horses looked brownish red, but not as bright as yours. The other horse looked much lighter."

"I still want my black stallion. If they can catch the horses, why can't we?" Juarez asked.

"They travel lighter and faster than us. No guns, armor, or food. They live really well without any of the stuff we've got."

"Yeah, but we've got our stuff. And they don't," Juarez said.

"I don't think they would want it," one of the men said.

"Why wouldn't they want it? Everybody wants it. Think what we did to get it."

"I don't think they would think it was worth it."

"You should watch your mouth. Do you want to go live with them?" Juarez asked.

"If I were as good at living off the land as they are, it would be interesting. In fact, it would be interesting to see how much we could do without."

"You're crazy. More is always better," Ponce said.

Juarez stopped in place without responding. He silently repeated the soldier's statement. He had never given any consideration to such a thought.

The man looked down at his boots and thought even his boots were ineffective here. He wanted to tell Ponce about how much he was enjoying all the stuff they had—which was not at all—but he didn't. He left that briefing envying the Natives' free spirits, resourcefulness, and casual attitudes. He went to his bunk, removed his boots, and spent the rest of the day wandering around the camp barefoot. The next day, he went to the beach barefoot and relished the feel of the sand between his toes. Within a week, four of his friends joined him on the beach in their off hours from the settlement. Not only did they dare to go barefoot, they began to collect seashells and took time to smell and enjoy the flowers. They began to see themselves as strangers in paradise.

Petnima and Gurefin talked with Manchun about the Spaniards one day as they made their way along a trail leading to a source of nuts and berries.

"Why do you think they're here?" Petnima asked.

"At first, I would have said it was for gold. Yes, I'm pretty sure they came looking for gold. Somehow, they've become fixated on pure water. How stupid can you get?"

Gurefin shook his head in bewilderment. "Sooner or later, even they will figure out that water is just water, and that there isn't much gold around here."

"Then what do you think they'll do?" Petnima asked.

"That's what worries me. We've been told by our seafaring friends about what they've done on some of the big islands out in the sea. It doesn't look like they're ever planning to leave. It's as if they think they need to control the land and everything they see."

"I'm not going to help them open their eyes. They might like what we could show them," Petnima said.

"Snakes, alligators, no pure water, no gold, and no friends, they might decide to leave," Gurefin said, then added, "Maybe we should lead them into snakes and alligators to help convince them."

"Let's let them figure it out for themselves. There seems to be a small group that find themselves at home on the sand and around the flowers. They seem to have some fun when they get those boots off," Manchun said.

The Spaniards, even without their good horse trainers, managed to get the four horses Targonsa returned trained to a point where they could ride them. The raw horses and the lack of saddles challenged them, but Ponce and Juarez were good riders. Ponce ordered one horse loaded with supplies while he, Juarez, and another rider started north and inland to look for horses. They spent the first night on the hills overlooking the marsh area where the snake bite occurred. There were no fresh signs of horses. Carrying long guns on a bareback horse was work all day and they were ready for a night's rest.

Targonsa and his friends with horses had managed to catch three more horses and more of their friends mastered bareback riding. They rode almost every day. They took turns riding and now, even with the additional horses, they had more riders than horses. They wanted more horses as much as the Spaniards wanted them. Ponce's red stallion and Juarez's black stallion had divided the remaining horses into two groups and the stallions moved their herds north and away from each other. The Natives traced the movements of the black stallion's herd of six mares, two of the original foals, and two brand new babies.

Three of Targonsa's friends rode the hilltops and found Ponce's campsite. They could only guess what Ponce's group was up to; they were looking for either pure water, gold, or horses. It was unlikely they'd try to find pure water on their own. There was no gold here, so they must be looking for horses. If that were the case, the Natives would not lead Ponce's group toward the black stallion.

The black stallion preferred the coastal side of the hills. The Natives decided to ride north on the marsh side and hoped the Spaniards would follow them. They rode out of sight around the Spanish camp until they knew the Spaniards would never catch them. On a high site they rode into an open hillside. When the Spaniards noticed them, the Natives began to "play bird with a bad wing and a nest in the opposite direction."

"Look at that, three of them on our horses," Juarez said.

"Let's pack this up and go see what they're up to," Ponce said. They piled camp supplies on the pack horse and climbed aboard their riding horses, armed with the long guns. Even without pulling a pack horse or carrying the long guns, they would never outride the Natives. Their only choice was to impatiently follow them. They towed the pack horse toward the open hillside. By midday, Ponce and company had achieved high ground above the open hillside. They scanned the area, only to watch the Natives disappear behind the next row of hills.

As the sun approached the horizon, the Natives rode on nearly level ground within sight of the Spaniards. They kept their distance until the Spaniards gave up and made a camp. "What do they want and why are they following us?" Junsrim asked.

"We're not going to let them near these horses. Let's lose them tomorrow."

"Let's lead them over the bridge. If these clouds let loose, they won't be able to get back without going all the way around. At least three days more to get back." A narrow half mile of solid ground bridged higher ground on each side of a large marsh and Junsrim knew that even a modest rain would put it under water. "We can lead them over it, ride around the big hill until the rain starts, then come back across.

If they follow us, they're so slow, it will flood before they get back." The Natives agreed and had a little chuckle over the plan.

As expected, when the Natives made themselves visible, the Spaniards rode toward them. Staying modestly ahead of the Spaniards and occasionally visible, all riders and horses made it across the bridge as the clouds gathered and the sky darkened. The big hill Junsrim had referred to appeared more like a small mountain that stood without company in the middle of an immense area of grassland raised above the marsh. All the ground around the marsh, and consequentially the bridge, served as a volatile watershed for the marsh. Four hours of riding managed to place the Natives halfway around the mountain. The Spaniards followed. As planned, it began to rain. Lightning and thunder added to the dramatics.

"I haven't seen any signs of loose horses out here," Ponce said.

"They're not out here for nothing," Juarez said.

"We're not going to find any gold out here either," Ponce said.

"No, no gold. It's got to be horses. We've got to let them lead us to the horses."

"You think they're leading us to the horses?" Ponce asked.

"They don't know they're leading us. We'll find them."

When Junsrim calculated that the Spaniards were halfway around the mountain, he urged his horse into a gallop and headed back to the bridge. By the time they reached the bridge, the watershed performed its ancient ritual and began to fill the marsh. The Natives rode easily across the bridge and then rested their horses as they watched the bridge disappear behind them. They rode a safe distance away from the marsh on a trail that allowed visual reconnaissance of the Spaniards' dilemma. The Spaniards followed the trail around the mountain. When they approached the marsh at sundown in the rain, the bridge no longer existed for them. They would spend a wet night in a camp they were not fully prepared for. The rain continued all the next day as well.

Junsrim and his band of happy riders decided to go all the way down to Manchun's small camp to say hello, tell the story of the Spaniards' plight, and talk to Targonsa about the horses. Knowing that the Spanish high command rode in unfamiliar territory and at least three days behind gave them confidence to ride straight onto the beach. They were surprised to see a few barefoot Spaniards walking peacefully in a light rain, and they smiled. Suddenly the clouds parted, the sun shone, and the Spaniards on the beach waved and smiled back to the Native riders. A pleasing change of attitudes, the Natives thought.

Four days later, a trio of horses with bedraggled riders stepped onto the beach in a mild warm rain. Four barefoot Spaniards casually watched the clouds change color as the sun approached the horizon. Ponce yelled to them, "Come get these horses."

"Where's the pack horse?" one of the barefoot Spaniards asked as he took the reins of Ponce's horse.

"She broke away in a thunderstorm."

"Get these horses in the compound and take care of them," Juarez said.

"Tell the cook to get a big meal ready in the mess hall," Ponce said.

Tomas, the third rider, handed his reins over and looked to Ponce and Juarez walking quickly toward the compound. He rolled his eyes and shook his head quietly. He said nothing. He didn't have to say anything. Failure oozed from every pore on the leaders' faces. No discussion ever surfaced during the expedition, but the third rider knew the truth. The Natives led them on a wild-goose chase and intentionally set up a long hard ride home. So much for paradise, with greed on your mind.

Ponce, Juarez, and Tomas sat at the table with unkempt hair and beards, their shoulders hunched over while they scooped a quick meal into their famished bodies.

"You made a good try to catch that mare," Juarez said to Tomas.

"If I hadn't tripped on that root, I would have had her."

"I want you to take a horse with three men to pick up the equipment we had to leave. I especially want the cooking pots and utensils. Be sure you get all the knives."

Not having any choice, Tomas said, "I'll leave tomorrow about midday. It should take about three days each way."

Ponce and Juarez retired to Ponce's cabin and poured rum in front of the fire.

"You ready to give up trying to find gold here and help me find the source of the water?"

"No. They got that gold from somewhere. I want to find it."

"Well, would you agree that it's not around here?"

"I think we'll have to mount an expedition to look a lot farther north."

"I think the water is up there too. Maybe we'll leave a small security force here to guard the ship and the settlement. We'll have to walk. We've only got three horses and that won't be enough for a thirty-day excursion."

"I don't see any other options. We've got two pigs curing in the smokehouse. Let's leave two days after Tomas gets back. We'll have to carry some supplies on our backs."

Ponce exhaled and added in a disappointed voice, "Okay."

CHAPTER 8

Juarez set about preparing for an extended excursion far to the north. He selected men capable of carrying heavy packs, machetes, knives, guns, and munitions. He supervised the packing of foodstuffs and utensils for his first major effort in the new world.

Ponce asked for a meeting with Manchun, which was granted. They met on the beach as a brilliant sunset spread out over the gulf waters.

"We're going to take many men and go north to explore the land."

"You've tried that a couple of times," Manchun said.

"This will be different."

"Oh, good. What will be different?"

"I'll be in charge and we'll be scouting ahead. Would you like to help?"

"What could we do?"

"Maybe show us the best trails. Maybe lend us a few horses."

"No. We're planning on going north for a while as well. Some of us will be riding horses. We need to refill our pure water."

"We'll be using our horses to carry supplies."

"Good luck. Perhaps we'll see you on the trail."

Ponce dejectedly trudged back to the settlement in faint moonlight. He gave in to considering the possibility of using brute force to take the horses. Then reality set in. Where were the horses? They never saw them in more than small groups and he couldn't identify any place where he knew he could find even one horse. The Natives were aloof and never gathered in more than small groups. If gold could be found, how would they find it? Most important, how would he ever find the Fountain of Youth without the Natives' help? No, a display of brute force risked losing more than it could ever achieve. Ponce hoped he could convince Juarez the consequences of violence would destroy everything.

Eventually, Tomas returned and reported the bad news. Their cache of equipment had disappeared. Their valuable cooking pots, utensils, and knives were now in the Natives' hands. That news forced Juarez to raid the ship's supply to stock the expedition. Ponce found it necessary to exert some power of command to quell Juarez's anger. By promising an opportunity to find gold, Ponce calmed him and got him back in line.

Ponce and Juarez walked through the compound gate, followed by thirty men. Some men wielded machetes to clear brush when necessary. The idea of following the Natives' trusty trails, although efficient, didn't fit with the Spaniards' concept of a straight line as being the shortest distance. Manchun had talked to him about that concept once. Ponce stubbornly rejected the advice even after Manchun told him a straight line was best only if you're a bird. Some men carried long swords and most men, including Ponce and Juarez, carried long guns. Three men towed three pack horses, fully loaded. Manchun and Petnima watched them disappear into the bushes, heading north and west, near the coast.

"An unfit leader, all that heavy stuff, and all those mouths to feed, it's going to be a slow walk," Petnima said.

"Other than on horseback, they're slow and clumsy. I'm glad we have the horses. Let's get all our horses and ride up to all others with horses. Then we'll ride north, well ahead of them. We'll warn everybody all the way to the Vortex," Gurefin said.

"I want to go. This could be fun."

"You're a good rider. Get Targonsa and let him know we should leave tomorrow."

Manchun, Petnima, Gurefin, and Targonsa rode off the beach at daylight. They followed a trail north and east toward Junsrim and his band with horses. They knew they could locate the Spaniards anytime. After two days of easy riding, Junsrim welcomed them to his horse camp. Around a small fire, Junsrim told Manchun they had four horses and ten people that rode with confidence. Then he added, "Bolsir has eight horses but only two riders. He caught the black stallion and his herd just a half day north. We are going there tomorrow to see how many are ready to ride." Manchun said the black stallion impressed him and that he knew how well trained he was. He told the camp about the Spaniards' plans and that the riders should go check out the herd. After they inspected the herd, they would decide on a plan to deal with the Spaniards.

The next afternoon at Bolsir's camp, Targonsa worked with each horse and made decisions about which horses were ready to ride north. The stallion made the go list. Two mares with foals would stay back and begin learning to get along with humans. Three of the remaining horses were ready to ride. The fourth mare required additional work, but that could happen as they moved north slowly.

Petnima swung herself up onto the stallion's back and rode as if they had worked together all their lives. She said she wanted to ride the stallion north. Bolsir had caught him, so it was up to him. He said it was impossible to deny that duo. Targonsa rode his red mare and Manchun stayed with his favorite horse. The other riders selected the unclaimed horses, and the horse patrol prepared to ride north and west, first to find the Spaniards, and then to remain far north of them. Manchun assumed Ponce had carefully considered a more organized and disciplined expedition. Other than a much larger force, he wondered what else Ponce intended for his sizable force.

They rode into several scattered camps, updated the residents regarding the Spaniards' general intentions, and asked if they had seen any sign of them. One camp near the coast said they had seen a three-person scouting party on horseback two days earlier. The Natives had circled back and discovered a large encampment where the Spaniards had erected tents. That makes sense for the Spaniards, Manchun thought. This time they're serious about exploring this new-to-them world. The horse patrol decided to find the current encampment and stay well away from the mounted scouting parties. The major encampment would move behind successful scouting forays. The horse patrol wouldn't have to monitor activities at the encampment if they kept tabs on the scouting parties.

Manchun's scouts remained invisible as they traced the newcomers' exploratory efforts. When the Spanish scouts explored areas the Natives knew ended in dead-ends, they left the Spanish scouts to figure it out for themselves. When the Spaniards happened upon a thoroughfare that led to the promised land, the Native scouts reported back and waited for the major encampment to fold up and follow the Spanish scouts' directives. After a few such moves, Manchun and Targonsa decided to ride close enough to communicate with the Spaniards. They exchanged little information, but the contact encouraged the Spaniards, except when they asked for pure water to treat rashes from some of the vines. When asked, Manchun told them they had run low on pure water and that they had to replenish the supply. Manchun knew the itches weren't fatal and decided to let them get over it on their own. It would diminish their effectiveness as a fighting force.

One Spanish scouting party included Juarez riding a minimally trained mare. He carried his long gun and rode from the encampment with two other riders, as Ponce demanded. They rode toward a row of hills due north. A half mile from the summit, Juarez watched as a horse and rider appeared on the skyline. He ordered the group to stop as he concentrated on the sight. The horse and rider moved in fluid congruency. No fast or jerky movements, just beautiful, well-placed steps in perfect harmony. He suspected the black horse to be his stallion. Finally, he focused and was sure Petnima rode his stallion.

"That woman is riding my stallion. Let's go." Juarez charged up the hill. Petnima watched the initial charge and vacated the hilltop. By the time Juarez and his group achieved the summit, Petnima and the stallion were riding peacefully along a trail in thick bushes. Juarez exhaled and knew that his current mount had no chance of ever catching Petnima. The Spanish crew rested their exhausted horses before they resumed the search for an acceptable route for the expedition.

When Juarez returned to the encampment, Ponce waited anxiously for route information, but Juarez was consumed with telling him about the black stallion. In time, Ponce extracted the information he needed and ordered a move the next day. Juarez insisted upon being allowed to join the scouting parties regularly. Ponce thought that would be a good way to be rid of him for at least a few hours most days.

Remarkably, even as slow as the Spaniards moved, the encampment had come to within a two-day ride of the Vortex. Despite an encouraging scouting report, however, the Spanish encampment remained in place due to an extended rainstorm. During the second day of rain, Juarez and two riders left camp and rode onto an almost-level rocky terrain with patches of low grass growing around the rocks. Manchun and six riders, concealed in surrounding bushes, watched them ride out.

After an hour and without warning, Juarez's horse reared, whirled, and jumped off the trail. A difficult task for a good rider in a saddle, but for a bareback rider on a raw horse, an impossible task. Juarez landed in a patch of grass, barely missing a large rock. He recovered to his hands and knees. Before he pushed himself up to a standing position, he yelled and shouted obscenities. He raised his left arm with a snake attached and grappled after the snake with his right hand. He pulled the snake off and killed it. He stood in silence, holding his left arm.

Manchun asked Targonsa to ride with him to the Spaniards. One of the Spaniards shouted to Manchun that a three-colored snake had bitten Juarez. Manchun approached and inspected the snake. He shouted to Targonsa that indeed it was a three-colored snake. Manchun's excitement and concern surprised Targonsa because they both knew that the king snake, although colored red, black, and yellow, wasn't poisonous. The sequence of colors made the difference between life and death. They knew perfectly well that only if the red and yellow bands touched each other was the snake poisonous. Targonsa, after a few seconds of puzzlement, jumped to. He shouted that he would ride to get some of the pure water.

"That's the same snake that killed one of my men. Are you telling me you can save me with your water?"

"We'll try if you want."

"Can't hurt, I guess," Juarez said.

Targonsa rode into the bushes and asked anyone for a small pouch of water. He took the pouch and told his friends to watch—it could be good. He rode at full speed to Manchun and handed him the pouch. Manchun slid off his horse and handed the reins to Targonsa. He went to Juarez and inspected the minor bite marks. He picked up a fist sized stone and scraped it hard against the wound.

"What are you doing?" Juarez asked.

"Opening it up so the pure water can work against the bite wound."

Minor bleeding creeped from Juarez's arm. "That hurts." Manchun applied the water so that it smothered the raw flesh. Then he took the rock and tapped firmly on Juarez arm below the wound. Again, Juarez said it hurt.

"That's good. If the pure water wasn't neutralizing the poison, you wouldn't be able to feel it." Manchun looked up to Targonsa and said he thought it was going to be okay. Targonsa smiled. He worked hard not to laugh out loud. Juarez stood on wobbly legs, believing that some portion of the poison affected his equilibrium. He asked another Spaniard to help him onto his horse. He said thank you. Manchun and Targonsa waved and rode back into the bushes.

When the Spaniards disappeared, the Natives had a good laugh about the gullibility they had witnessed. But then, what else would they have believed? The Spaniards' return to camp proved more somber. The riders slid off the horses in front of Ponce's tent. A solemn return, but the scout excitedly told Ponce the story of how Manchun saved Juarez. "The three-colored snake bit him, and Manchun with pure water saved him. He's alive. The water worked."

"Is that right?" Ponce asked.

"Yes. That's right."

"I knew it, I knew it. What do you think about the water now?"

"I'd like to know how much more it can do," Juarez answered.

"Do you think it's more valuable than your gold?"

"If I live through this, I will say yes."

"Good. Some lessons come hard. Remember, we'll need the Indians to find the source."

CHAPTER 9

Ponce looked out from his tent and watched the rain, pleased that Juarez would likely survive, and even more pleased that Juarez joined him in believing in the water's value. He stepped out from the protective roof. He smiled and looked up to the heavens. Time after time the pure water proved its medicinal values. He stood on the brink of immortality. The Fountain of Youth beckoned. A shrine at the source, in his name, welcoming royalty forevermore. The most important people in the world would travel to his temple and pay homage to him. He allowed himself to visualize his castle on a hill overlooking the gurgling spring of pure water. Yes, kings and even popes would ask for an audience in the grand ballroom. He didn't have to find any gold; they would bring it to him. He would dress in the finest clothes and eat the finest foods. It was all within reach. He thought that soon he would call the sergeant to give the order to move the encampment over the route the scouts had described.

Then reality set in. He was soaking wet and admitted that he didn't know how to find the source. How could he encourage the Indians to divulge the trail to the source? Ponce decided to consult Juarez. Juarez was clever and now that he too believed, Ponce had an ally.

"Yes, we can move the encampment, we have a route we know is good for at least a full day's ride. But . . . where are we going?" Juarez asked.

"We're going to the source," Ponce responded confidently.

"Well that's great. Where is it? We've seen the results of the water. We think it's somewhere here in the north. The Indians have never told anybody about a specific location."

"They get it from somewhere. I'm sure it's near here. I think we're close."

"Well . . . again . . . that's great. Now tell me how we find it."

"We'll know it when we see it. I know we will."

"What? Do you expect to hear music playing, have the rain cease, have the sun stop in the sky and shine upon you?" Juarez asked indignantly.

"We'll know when we find it."

"I think we better have a plan. We need the Indians."

"They've always talked about it being up north."

"They've always avoided answering any questions about the water. What if they've led us on another wild-goose chase? What if the source is south?"

"It's here. I know it is. It has to be," Ponce said insistently.

"I think we need to ask Manchun some hard questions about the source."

"Well, do you want to ride out and try to find him?"

"I think it's our only choice. Do you want to stay here and hope to contact Manchun, or do you want to move the camp?"

"Let's have the men move the camp on foot with one horse. You and I can ride out in front, ready to talk if Manchun comes out of the bushes," Ponce said.

In the morning, Ponce issued orders to move the camp. He and Juarez rode out to follow the scouts' trail. Ponce and Juarez talked openly about how the pure water had benefited them. The discussion drove home their opinions. Their resolve to find the source intensified as they each confirmed the other's belief. The sun also brightened their spirits. Their positive attitudes completely disregarded the remote possibility that Manchun would never show up. Neither did they devise a plan B if Manchun refused to divulge or even discuss the source. Optimism shepherded their course.

From a highpoint at midday, they looked back and watched a long line of men carrying camp supplies to the promise of immortality. The two remained optimistic, although they failed to contact Manchun or a representative. They continued to ride in the open, hoping the Natives would decide to approach. Late in the afternoon, they gave up and retraced the trail to join the men as they rebuilt the camp.

Juarez asked Ponce if he thought maybe Manchun refused to join them while they carried their guns. Ponce liked the security of a gun and told Juarez that. Juarez put the guns into perspective.

"With two guns, we get two shots off, then a rain of arrows falls on us. That's a false sense of security." Ponce thought about it and failed to answer immediately.

Juarez drove his point home. "If we can't convince them to trust us, they're not likely to co-operate when it comes to leading us to the source." Ponce responded by agreeing to ride out in the morning without his gun. He decided to leave the camp in place until they made contact and received some direction from the Indians.

The sight of two Spaniards out of camp without guns indeed influenced the Natives. When Ponce and Juarez rode onto an open area with no cover, Manchun, Gurefin, Petnima, and Targonsa rode from their obscured positions to greet them.

"How are your travels?" Manchun asked, knowing that carrying supplies on their backs in the rain took a lot of fun out of exploring.

"We're seeing some new country. We'd like to find the source of the pure water," Ponce answered.

"How's the snake bite?"

"Good as ever. Thank you, again," Juarez answered.

"How much further north are you going?"

"Maybe until we find the source," Ponce answered.

"How will you know when you find it?" Manchun asked.

Ponce focused on the ground in front of his horse, then answered, "Don't know. Will you help us?"

"It's a quiet place of peace."

"Seems like that's where pure water should come from."

"What if you find it and are disappointed?"

"Don't know why we'd be disappointed. We've seen how good it is."

"Things are seldom what they seem. That's all I can tell you now. We must get back."

"Can we talk about it?"

"We'll meet you here tomorrow." The Natives galloped off the open area and disappeared into the bushes.

"What are we going to tell them tomorrow?" Petnima asked.

"Something that will leave them wanting more," Gurefin said.

"They always want more. They seem to be set on finding the source," Targonsa said.

"They wouldn't know it if they drown in it," Gurefin said.

"What can we extract from them if we agree to lead them to the Vortex?" Petnima asked.

"They want it. They're not even talking about gold anymore—just pure water," Manchun said.

"Their guns, swords, and machetes make me nervous. I fear they are too willing to fight to take our horses. Their lifestyle depends upon them," Targonsa said.

"Our lives are better with them too," Petnima said as she patted her big black stallion on his neck and shoulder.

"You told them it came from a quiet place of peace. What can we do with that?" Gurefin asked.

"Let's try to keep it peaceful. I'd like to give them every reason to want it." Manchun studied each of his companions and recognized the concern on their faces. He faced the same concern. Once the Spaniards had the source, the Natives lost control over them. They could outride the Spaniards without saddles, they could still eat from the land and sea, and they still had potions and remedies for minor disorders. Those skills and knowledge gave them advantages over the Spaniards, but the gullibility factor based on the pure-water mysteries remained fixed in place only if they continued to chase nebulous thoughts and sought the unknown. "How can we manufacture another crisis that the pure water will solve?"

"Don't know. No stingrays here. I don't want to seek out and play with snakes. By now even they know enough to stay out of the sumac and poison ivy."

"Can't imagine how the water would fix an alligator attack," Petnima said.

"Maybe less is more," Targonsa whispered. He went silent and closed his eyes. No one spoke for several seconds.

"What do you mean?" Gurefin asked.

"Well . . . I just threw something out. Something that by itself has no meaning. You want more. Right?"

"That's what Manchun has been doing with them," Petnima said.

"I know. Unless or until we're handed some crisis to solve, let's intensify the mystery for them until they're ready to join us in a peaceful life."

"Let's always be prepared to deepen the mystery," Manchun said.

"We should strive for peace," Targonsa said.

Ponce and Juarez rode toward their camp hopeful but disappointed.

"They're willing to talk to us," Ponce said.

"We'll go back tomorrow, again without guns."

Ponce stopped his horse and thought a bit. "Should we bring a gift for them tomorrow?"

"Maybe we can trade something for guiding us to the source. What do you have in mind?"

"They seemed to like the roast pig. Let's take a piece of the ham tomorrow."

"Let's see what that gets us," Juarez said, not all that enthusiastically. Then he obstinately added, "That woman is still riding my stallion."

"I don't think she's going to give him up."

"After we find the source, after that, I'll get him back."

Ponce wanted all the horses back too, but he worried that Juarez would dwell on his obsession over the stallion and disrupt delicate negotiations. He told him to be patient and remember the source was their destiny. Juarez admitted that Ponce spoke the truth but added that he would never have another horse like the stallion. Ponce reminded him that the woman rode the stallion well, in fact as well as any Spanish rider. Juarez also had to admit that.

Ponce slept soundly and awoke with a positive attitude. Not that he had achieved anything the previous day, but at least he hadn't been told no. He cut a half pound of ham from the precious delicacy and placed it in a metal box. He and Juarez went to the grooms and climbed aboard two of the three horses still controlled by the Spaniards. Ponce gripped the box with ham and considered how he could propose a trade. He debated whether he should simply present a gift, or if he could contrive the situation into a trade for the information he obsessed over. Juarez wondered if he could affect a trade for the stallion.

Gurefin noticed that Ponce held something in one hand as he rode. Manchun wondered about it. The Spaniards sat upon their horses alone at the designated spot. Manchun said he was curious and began to ride slowly to the meeting. Petnima worked the stallion with her heels and the reins to display a well-disciplined high-stepping walk.

Juarez noted the riding ability required to work the stallion effectively. Face-to-face, Manchun asked how the people in the camp were doing. He intentionally let it be known that he concerned himself with the well-being of all individuals, not only the leaders in front of him.

Juarez stared at Petnima until her eyes met his. When her eyes locked onto his eyes, he smiled and nodded his head approvingly. Petnima smiled back, acknowledging that he approved of her riding. Juarez wanted gold and the water, but he respected her talent for riding.

"We brought you some of a pig we specially prepared," Ponce said.

"We brought nothing to trade for it. We can't take it," Manchun said.

"We want you to have it." Ponce hesitated and watched Manchun's expression.

Manchun failed to respond.

To the point, Juarez said, "You could lead us to the source."

Manchun reached for the ham and said, "Tomorrow we'll bring you something for the pig meat."

Ponce released the box with a stunned look on his face. At once he realized Manchun had outplayed him again. He went into a self-introspection mode:

How could this be happening? I am educated from an advanced society, I can speak Latin, I have had a personal relationship with a king and a queen. How can an ignorant Native get away with this?

He watched carefully as the Indians rode slowly into the bushes. He continued to stare well after they disappeared.

"Ponce. Ponce? Are you okay?" Juarez asked.

"How is this happening to us?"

"What's that?"

"Again, we get nothing. What do we have to do?"

Juarez, still impressed with Petnima's riding, said nonchalantly, "Let's see what they bring us tomorrow."

"You mean mañana. And what if mañana never comes?"

"You sound like you want to quit," Juarez said.

"No. Not quit, but I want some movement."

Manchun asked Gurefin to get a large alligator and slow-cook the tail with smoke all night. He said he had to respond to the Spaniards' surprise gift. Gurefin tasked individuals and satisfied Manchun that the alligator would be ready in the morning.

Slices of slow-cooked alligator tail flavored with local spices and herbs graced a large wooden platter. Manchun mounted up, took the platter, and led the way to the daily meeting. Targonsa, Petnima, and Gurefin followed. Their long black hair flowed gracefully in the light breeze. Ponce watched the proud people riding tall with self-confidence. He resented their control. He thought it should be him, riding his red stallion, dressed in shiny armor, and claiming this land under his governorship for Spain. Today the thought of eternal fame, based upon finding the Fountain of Youth, failed to brighten his disposition. Juarez concentrated on Petnima and the black stallion, riding assertively, in complete control with no visible cues to precisely command the powerful stallion. He watched and speculated on what it would take to strike a deal. Manchun rode up and stopped next to Ponce. He presented the wooden platter to him.

"I think you'll enjoy this as much as we enjoyed the pig."

Targonsa, Petnima, and Gurefin stopped their horses on a line, side by side, facing Juarez and Ponce. Manchun guided his horse to the end of the line next to Gurefin. Juarez spoke first.

"What will it take to find the pure water source?"

"I greatly fear you would be disappointed if we took you there. Remember, I told you that things are seldom what they seem," Manchun answered.

"But why should we not go there?"

"It is our place of peace and well-being. We go there to heal ourselves, to think, to refresh, to study, and to learn."

"We can respect that," Juarez said.

Ponce smiled. At least dialogue, he thought.

"Can you? Power, conflict, intolerance, and fighting are not permitted there."

"Do you think we are incapable of compatible behavior?"

"I only know what I have observed."

"We have some problems. I'll admit that, but we might be better than you think."

"I'm sure you both are capable of demonstrating impeccable behavior during a visit, but . . . but what about the next day? And how will your men behave? How will they treat our people studying there in peace? I worry about those things."

"Yes, I can see that." Juarez looked to Ponce, who perceived a process for a breakthrough solution to the problem at hand. Manchun waited for Ponce to join the conversation. Finally, Ponce looked to Manchun.

"We can promise you that we will respect your people there," Ponce said.

"Your promises are no good to us. We have seen you break promises and try to back out of agreements."

Once again, Ponce didn't like being called on his personal behavior. He maintained his composure and tried to swallow the truth Manchun spoke. Juarez's only opportunity to continue the negotiations depended on him taking the lead from Ponce. "What would you require of us to convince you to trust us?"

"One step forward would be for you to prove *you* trust *us*," Gurefin said.

"We're willing to discuss that path."

"If you gave up your weapons, it would be one of your steps on that path."

Ponce shuddered and quickly looked to Juarez as if to ask, "What are you doing?" Juarez stroked his beard and tried to digest all the implications. Ponce waited in silent anticipation. Surely Juarez would never surrender their guns and swords. The Natives, always alert, noted Ponce's response. They wondered how closely the Spaniards had coordinated their parts in this scene.

"How would we defend ourselves?" Juarez asked.

"Defend yourselves from what?" Manchun asked.

And yet again, Manchun managed to ask the important, although embarrassing, question. Juarez stared at the ground. Then at Ponce. Then he extended his arm and swept it halfway around him indicating the countryside. "There are a lot of dangerous animals out there."

"How often have you used your weapons to defend yourselves from them?" Targonsa asked.

Manchun rolled his eyes to Ponce and silently demanded an answer. Ponce shifted his weight and looked away before he admitted that it had not been necessary to use the guns to defend themselves. Then he added, "If our men had guns with them, the bears would not have killed them, and our horses would not have escaped."

"We don't need guns to keep bears away. Maybe you could learn some new ways before you kill something or someone," Gurefin said.

"We don't bring our guns when we come talk to you," Ponce said.

Juarez quickly devised a solution to ease the tensions about the guns. He raised his hand and opened his mouth, but Petnima cut him off.

"Tomorrow you could march thirty men out here with guns."

Manchun nodded agreement with Petnima's statement and noted that Juarez had something to say. "Yes, carry on."

"Never mind."

Ponce failed to catch the nuance of Petnima's statement, as Juarez had done. "Suppose we leave all the guns in camp when we go to the source?"

"What does that solve?" Gurefin answered.

"No one would get shot at the source," Ponce said.

"Only that day. I think we should leave," Gurefin said as he turned his horse away.

Before Targonsa and Petnima could follow, Juarez asked if they could think about it overnight and meet again.

"Do you have something substantial you are considering, or are you wasting our time?" Manchun said. He recognized an opportunity to tell the Spaniards who was in control.

"We need to talk," Juarez said.

"Okay, we'll try tomorrow."

Before Petnima turned to leave, she backed her stallion three steps and winked at Juarez. Juarez smiled.

Back at the camp, Juarez said, "We need to talk about this whole situation. Let's put these horses away and take a walk down by the river."

"You sound like you want to make a major decision."

"You're in command, but let's talk about it."

Juarez led Ponce down a short trail to a grassy bank where they could watch the clear water in the small river drift peacefully. Occasionally a leaf or flower floated by. An agitated Ponce set his eyes on Juarez, who smiled at the scene.

"Sit down Ponce, relax."

"What are we going to do? We must do something."

"Let's talk about our options. What can we do?"

"We could take a few prisoners," Ponce said, almost without thinking.

"And then what happens?"

"We trade them for information."

"What if they refuse? Are you willing to kill the hostages?"

"Why not? I wouldn't want to, but I'm the governor."

"And if you kill somebody, what happens next?"

"I don't know."

"We have to know. We need an exit strategy. You were trained in military tactics. You know these things," Juarez said.

"I selected you for your help when it comes to a fight."

"I can fight a just fight. But Ponce . . . I'm tired of fighting. Look at the sight before you. Clear water, flowers, peace; it's a beautiful thing."

"You can be tired after we secure the source."

"I would like to see the source too, but I don't think we're going to see it by fighting."

"How's that going to happen then?" Ponce asked.

Juarez leaned back and closed his eyes. He let his mind drift back to his childhood. He grew up poor, in an impoverished coastal village. He reminisced about being barefoot on the shore. How he picked mussels and whelks from the rocks and how much he liked the octopus when he could catch them. He considered his transition from a happy childhood to a man ready to fight to gain more. "Why can't we just join these people and enjoy this beautiful land?" He wondered if he intentionally let that statement slip out.

"They will never get that close to us as long as we have our guns."

"Well?"

"Well what? You're not considering giving them our guns?"

"Why not? They've got hundreds of people out there plus some horses. We've got thirty men and three horses. They could easily starve us out without ever being seen if they wanted to. What good are the guns then?" Juarez asked.

Ponce rested his elbows on his knees and held his head. Juarez watched the river. Ponce realized that he was running out of options. His mind raced. He panicked. His quest for the source overrode all consideration. He was out of control. "Okay, okay, okay. I'll negotiate with our guns tomorrow. I need the source."

"Tomorrow might be our last chance. Did you notice their attitude today?"

"I'll do it."

CHAPTER 10

Juarez remained conscious late into the night. He had said to Ponce, "I'm tired of fighting." He hadn't thought a lot about it before he said it. Now he wondered if he could be fully committed to a life of peace. The Natives seemed to be happy without looking for a fight. He thought about how he had wanted to join the men from the settlement as they walked barefoot on the beach. He knew he wanted to be barefoot on the beach too, but he also knew his position forbade it. He wished he'd done it, even just once.

He came here prepared to fight for gold so that he could impress a woman. How much gold did he need? How much did Ponce need? How much did the people in Spain need? He thought they would never have enough. Perhaps everybody possessed the same amount: "not quite enough." Regardless how much they had, they always wanted more. The Natives here didn't fit that mold. They had everything they needed or wanted—food, water, beauty, peace, and tranquility.

Juarez considered the charges he had accepted as a Spanish military man. The weight of those responsibilities pushed him along a path with few options. The oppression of obeying orders without a serious voice for objection weighed upon him. But then, his position offered certain positive perks as well. He had a tent of his own, better food than most, wine, rum, and a percent of the gold they found. Was it worth it? What if he could go barefoot and pick nuts, berries, and coconuts when he felt like it? How would it feel to wear flowers around his neck? Oh well, he thought, it wasn't going to happen. But the concept of it gave him some relief from his responsibilities, even if only for a few minutes.

Ponce struggled with sleep and reentered the world less than ready. Juarez, on the other hand, appeared in a clean shirt and a well-trimmed beard. At the appointed time, Ponce rode with Juarez to the open meeting ground. Petnima always wore a sleeveless leather top to the meetings, and today she sported a new one. The two factions aligned themselves facing each other. Ponce announced that he wished to negotiate with the guns.

"I think you will like what my commander has to say," Juarez said. Then he caught Petnima's eye and motioned for her to join him. Juarez moved his horse away from Ponce while Petnima backed her horse from between Targonsa and Gurefin and walked him to join Juarez twenty feet from the meeting.

"Can we take a short ride together?" Juarez asked.

Petnima thought that was an odd request for Juarez to make but also thought she would like to learn more about the man and the Spaniards' intentions. "Why not?" They walked their horses slowly away from the group.

"That horse you're riding belonged to me before we lost all the horses."

"I thought so. I watched you ride him on the beach."

"Do you think they'll agree on a plan to go the source?"

"It's possible. I know the weapons were a big deal. I hope you're not disappointed."

"After what the water has done for us, I can't imagine how we would be disappointed."

"Remember what Manchun said—things are seldom what they seem."

"But—"

"Things are seldom what they seem."

"Why are you so guarded about it?"

"It's an important place for us. We go there to refresh, study, learn, and just relax."

"But the water?"

"Things are seldom what they seem."

"Where do you go when it rains?"

"Same place we go when the sun shines."

"But you get all wet."

"And then we get dry. It's just water."

"I wonder if I could ever be that free."

"You've got too much stuff."

"It makes our lives better."

"Does it? Everything we need is right here. We just take it when we need it, fresh."

"I wonder if I could learn to live like that."

"You won't appreciate the source until you do."

Juarez thought about that statement. He also believed he understood the implications. Without stuff, and the need for more stuff, and the need to protect and secure the stuff, the Natives cherished the world before them. They didn't find it necessary to pick a flower to enjoy it. They didn't take ten oysters if they only needed five. Why couldn't he leave his stuff?

"Thanks for the insights. Let's ride back to see what happened."

They approached the group in time to hear Gurefin say, "And how will we know when we have all the guns?"

"Every man has a long gun, and Juarez and I each have a spare as well."

"I would feel better if one of us could also come into your camp to check."

"I will escort one or more through the camp," Juarez said.

"Is that okay now?" Ponce asked of the Natives.

"That will work. We will be here in this open space to remove the guns in the morning. Then Juarez can take Targonsa and Gurefin into the camp. Then we will take you two to the source."

Juarez rode next to Ponce on the return to camp. "I don't want to be part of broken promises. Will you assure me that all the guns are turned over? Don't embarrass me by having them find a gun in the camp," Juarez said.

"Don't worry, we'll get all the arquebuses. Of course, they will have no powder or balls."

"What if the source isn't everything you expect?"

"Well, then we'll know, won't we?" Ponce slid off his horse and sent the word out that all guns must be brought to his tent immediately.

Manchun and his companions joined their friends at their camp. They hobbled the horses and walked to a small waterfall that trickled into a quiet pool.

"That just seemed too easy," Gurefin said.

"They really want the water," Manchun said.

"We'll find out why tomorrow," Targonsa said.

"They are going to be disappointed. I repeated what you told them, 'things are seldom what they seem.' Juarez seemed to be interested in how we respect the area," Petnima said.

"I'm really concerned about their reaction after they see nothing more than clear water flowing out of the ground," Manchun said.

"What if they chase our people away and build a fence around it?" Targonsa asked.

"We won't let that happen. They've got thirty men skilled with swords and knives. We've got five times that many with arrows and camouflage. I hope it doesn't come to that."

"It'll be about a two-hour ride. There's nothing else, so we'll take them and bring them back," Targonsa said.

"Oh yes. We must take some men to the meeting to carry the guns away. I will tell them to assure they are well-dispersed and hidden. Then, I will advise them to watch the Spaniards in their camp until we return."

Ponce's big day arrived with clear skies and a light breeze. To avoid any delays, his first order of business centered on removing the guns and depositing them in the open area. He ordered ten men to carry all the guns out of the camp. He silenced one dissenting voice and ordered his men to stay in camp until he returned.

Ponce and Juarez mounted their horses and walked them slowly to the pile of guns on the ground. Manchun and his riding companions entered the open area from four separate locations. They all convened at the pile of guns.

"Are you ready for our people to come collect the guns?" Manchun asked.

"They're all yours," Juarez answered.

Manchun motioned to the bushes and twelve men entered the open area, moving toward the group. He counted thirty-four long guns and asked his men to carry them away. They did that without hesitation.

Ponce's thoughts of the Fountain of Youth so overpowered him that he couldn't consider the long-term consequences of giving up the guns. His sole concern consumed him.

"Are you ready to inspect the camp?" Ponce asked, quickly.

"You promised thirty-four guns and they're all here. I don't think we need to bother your camp today. Shall we ride now? It will take us about two hours."

"Let's go," Ponce said. Targonsa led the group, Manchun and Ponce rode side by side, Juarez rode up next to Petnima, and Gurefin followed. A half hour of easy riding with light conversation brought them to a steep rocky mountainside with a minimal trail. Targonsa asked Ponce and Juarez if they would rather walk the horses up and over the mountainside. They declined and continued slowly. At the summit, they took a break to rest the horses and to survey the landscape.

To the west, from the base of the mountain, miles of grasslands extended atop a mild plateau, which in turn sat above lush forests. The forests extended to the north as far as they could see. To the east of the summit, the forest gave way to smaller trees and bushes which extended to the south from which they rode. Manchun pointed west and said their destination rested at the far end of the grasslands. Juarez said the view from the summit made the trip worthwhile by itself.

Ponce stared at the grasslands. An easy hour to ride through the grasslands and he would fulfill his destiny. He went into trancelike deep meditation, considering the priest's prophecy. He had done it. He was the connection between the infamous Fountain of Youth and kings, queens, popes, and all of Europe. Visions of fame and immortality filled his head. Ponce remained in that mental state and began to whisper to himself; words, more like babble, escaped his lips.

Petnima reached out and touched Juarez's arm. He looked to her and she motioned for him to fall back and ride with her away from the group. She said she wanted to show him another sight. She guided Juarez to the plateau edge that overlooked the area where the forest transformed to lands with small trees and bushes. She pointed out a waterfall as the river ran over the edge of the forest and into the bushes. She told him that it was the river that ran close to their camp and that it came from the source. Without specific reference to the water, Juarez studied the scene and commented on the overall beauty of the landscape. "Peace," he whispered.

"Are you concerned about having no guns?" Petnima was determined to pry into Juarez's thought processes.

"I'm trying not to think about it."

"Do you think it makes you vulnerable to us?"

"Nothing I've seen from your people makes me feel vulnerable."

"You haven't had to use them to protect yourselves from any of the animals."

"That's true."

"There's only one other reason you would want them, then," Petnima said.

"Do you mean to use them to conquer you and your people?"

"I guess that's everybody's concern."

"In that case, I'm glad they're gone. I suppose I hadn't worked that all the way through."

"We've heard about what the Spaniards have done on some of the islands. We've been on guard."

"I hope the water doesn't push Ponce too far. Let's enjoy this scene while we can."

They studied the scene, mostly in silence, until they had to gallop the horses to meet the other riders close to the source.

As they approached the other riders, they slowed the horses to a quiet walk. "Thank you. When I stop to look at things here, I seem to calm down and find some inner peace," Juarez said.

"It's good for you."

"Let's do it again soon."

"Okay."

The riders entered a grove of loosely spaced oak trees. Manchun led the group single file through the oak forest. When he exited the grove, he stopped and faced the other riders. "This is the source; we call it the Vortex. More about that in a while. Please respect it. You will encounter children, students, elders, and elderly people. Please don't disturb them."

Ponce and Juarez looked out over fifty yards of green flowing grass between them and an elongated pool of perfectly clear water. At the far-right end of the pool, the water flowed effortlessly into a small river. On the far side of the pool, undulating grassy knolls between the water and tall trees provided the Natives natural congregation areas. Several groups of from three to about a dozen individuals sat and interacted congenially. Neither Ponce nor Juarez spoke. Ponce appeared spellbound. Juarez looked to Petnima and nodded approvingly. Finally, Ponce said, "I want to drink the water."

"Let's tie the horses in the trees and all have a drink," Gurefin said.

Ponce instantly dismounted and led his horse into the trees. Impatiently, he waited for his companions to follow. He managed to restrain himself from breaking ranks and running to the water. When all six newcomers reached the pool, Ponce knelt with both knees in the cool water and cupped water in his hands. Almost ceremoniously, he raised the water over his head, allowed it to flow through his fingers, and let it fall into his mouth. With his knees still in the pool, he sat up straight with his arms folded across his chest, and with his eyes closed, he began a slow, low, incomprehensible chant. Juarez and the Natives cupped water in their hands and enjoyed a refreshing drink. Petnima rose and led Juarez away from Ponce. Manchun, Targonsa, and Gurefin also walked away from Ponce, still in an apparent trance, to take reconnaissance of the people on the opposite side of the pool.

Petnima motioned toward Ponce. "Is he okay?"

"He has some emotional tie to that water. I have seen what it can do, but he is obsessed with it. I don't understand it."

"Perhaps I shouldn't say anything, but it's just . . . I hope you're not disappointed," Petnima said.

"But . . . the stingray, poisonous plants, and snake bites?"

"Not now; just don't be disappointed."

"Disappointed? How could anybody be disappointed with this? Here, I feel . . . I feel almost free."

"Free from what?"

"I don't know, maybe free of obligations and responsibilities from the old world."

"Come, I'll take you for a walk to see the other side."

Ponce opened his eyes, cupped more water, and poured handful after handful over his face. When he considered himself properly cleansed, he stood and studied the vicinity in detail. He thought, this place, the trees, the green grass, the fresh air, the water, yes, the water, this is what the priest had promised me. I've done it, I have it, the world is mine. Then Ponce surveyed the landscape. The high ground behind the minor undulations would be perfect for his mansion—not a castle with high walls and small windows, but a palace with verandas and open-air areas where popes and kings would pay homage. Cleansed in pure water from the Fountain of Youth, Ponce and his guests would dress in the finest linens and silk. They would feast on the finest foods and drink the best wines from the old world, and of course rum, Ponce continued to fantasize. Oblivious to the people on the opposite shore or his recent companions, Ponce began to shuffle his feet into a small dance, faced the sky, spread his arms, and spun in minute circles. In utter ecstasy, he finally collapsed onto his back in the grass. He extended his arms, closed his eyes, and visualized his destiny.

Petnima led Juarez along a trail beyond the lower end of the pool. The calm clear river water expanded into an ideal pool for swimmers and children. Long rock slabs tilted gently from the riverbank into the river to provide easy access. At the lower end of the pool, water flowed out over a two-foot waterfall. Natives swam and children played in the shallow end of the pool. "When you're ready, your friends can come here to bathe and wash clothes over there where the water flows over the edge," Petnima said.

Juarez considerately asked, "Is there a good time when we won't interfere with your people?"

"Early in the morning might be best."

"Everyone will be happy with this. I'll schedule it. I'm sure Ponce will want to move the camp here for a while." Juarez thought to himself that he would make every effort to remind the men that they would be guests here. Juarez followed Petnima back up the trail to where they left Ponce.

Gurefin watched Petnima and Juarez walking in a relaxed manner on the trail and wondered what had changed. He knew Petnima would never waste time with Juarez unless she recognized a substantial change in attitude. He was curious and wanted to ask her about it.

Gurefin told Manchun they should check on Ponce and get ready for the ride back. Ponce paced along the edge of the pool, stopping periodically to survey the view and memorizing every aspect. Manchun approached Ponce and asked if he was satisfied.

Ponce responded with a huge smile. "Yes, just as I expected."

"I hope you don't find too much disappointment. Remember, things are seldom what they seem," Manchun said.

Juarez and Petnima heard the conversation from a distance on the trail. "When you're ready, will you tell me why I keep hearing that things are seldom what they seem?"

"In due time." They continued to walk toward the others.

"Are you ready to start back, Juarez?" Gurefin asked.

"I think we should do that. Are you ready, Ponce?"

"I don't want to leave, but we'll be back."

Before they left the pool, Manchun pointed to a rock face rising from the left edge of the pool. "The water is deep beneath that rock. There is a cave deep under the water—do not swim into the cave."

"Are there alligators?" Ponce asked.

"No, but there is a river that will carry you away. Don't go there."

Ponce digested the comments and found it difficult to believe that in this peaceful pool there could be a strong underground river current.

He wondered what the cave hid. Ponce carried that thought to the horses waiting in the trees. The riders mounted up and began the walk back to the Spanish encampment. Within minutes Ponce said, "I want to move the camp up here as soon as possible."

"We don't allow camping at the pool. Day use only," Manchun said.

"Where can we camp?"

"In the field, on the far side of these trees, or you can go down the river below the canyon, but that's a hard climb to the upper river and pools." They rode on through the trees while Ponce internally calculated distances and access. As they exited the grove and the grassland extended before them, Manchun said, "As long as you stay out of the trees, you can set up a temporary camp on this grassland. It must be temporary. We don't allow long-term camps anywhere near the Vortex."

Without speaking, Ponce acknowledged that Manchun had provided guidelines for an encampment. Given his experiences on Hispaniola, Puerto Rico, and other islands, he assumed the wishes of the Natives were only a minor inconvenience until he could take what he wanted. He knew what he wanted.

Gurefin wanted to know more about the Spaniards' intentions. He motioned for Juarez to follow him away from the other four riders. When they were able to carry on a private conversation, Gurefin asked, "What are Ponce's intentions now?"

"I'm not sure. I know we both wanted to come to the source to understand what has served us well. It's a beautiful place and I will do everything I can to see that the men respect it and your wishes."

"I may have misjudged you. At one time I recognized you as aggressive and greedy. If I was wrong, I apologize."

"No, you weren't wrong. I had personal reasons for greed, and I wanted everything I could get. Your demeanor, the flowers, and the general atmosphere has made me realize that there is something more important than greed and control."

"What about the water?"

"On the surface, it appears that the water helped us many times. I have also heard, many times, that things are seldom what they seem. I'm beginning to wonder if it's the water or something in the water."

"What about Ponce and the water?"

"He still believes the water is magic. He has never questioned that."

"I just hope your men will respect our people that go there for quiet deliberation. You won't see them at the pools, but warriors are not far away, and they will fight, if necessary."

"I don't want to fight, and you have our guns."

"Ponce seems to be obsessed with the Vortex. Should we be concerned about his intentions?"

"He has life-and-death control over all of us. If any of us fight him, we could never go back to the ship. I've never seen him so consumed with anything like he was at the pools today. Yes, I will tell you, I am concerned about him."

"We'll be watching. Thank you for talking with me. And you're right—things are seldom what they seem. Let's ride back."

Ponce sat on his horse and let it carry him home. He wasn't riding, he was a passenger. He remained silent and held his head high in the air, but in the clouds would better describe the picture. He remained oblivious to the trail, grass, trees, sky, or his companions. His reflections revolved entirely around his life after he totally controlled all the land around the Vortex.

Juarez appeared consumed in thought as well. He knew he spoke the truth to Gurefin—Ponce was obsessed. He hoped he could avoid conflicts to maintain the peace. Those thoughts circulated until the group reached the compound.

CHAPTER 11

The Natives left Ponce and Juarez at their camp and rode off to rejoin their friends who had been monitoring the Spanish camp. "I think we may have misjudged Juarez," Petnima said.

"I've been talking with him. I believe he wants to get along with us."

"I talked to him as well," Gurefin said. "I admitted that I had thought he was aggressive and greedy when we first met, but that I recognized a different man now. Then I apologized for my first impressions. He told me our first impressions were correct and that he hoped he could prove that he had changed. Furthermore, he also is concerned about Ponce. I believe he will try to keep Ponce under control."

"That sounds like the man I've been talking to."

"What does he think Ponce will do?" Manchun asked.

"He doesn't know. He says Ponce is obsessed with the water—beyond reason," Gurefin said.

"I think all the people with horses should flank the Spaniards when they move their camp," Targonsa said.

"That, and let's ask the archers to be available too, just in case we can't keep the peace. Even without their guns, their body armor, long swords, and knives could make them a formidable force," Manchun said.

"There are only thirty-two of them and they only have three horses. If we have trouble, the first thing we should do is get those horses. I wonder what Juarez will do," Petnima said.

"We won't cause trouble, but we must be firm," Manchun said.

Back at the Spanish camp, Ponce, Juarez, and two commanders, José and Pedro, met near the river where Ponce could draw sketches in the sand. He selected a stick and reconstructed the layout at the Vortex. He had burned the images into his brain and his rendering proved exquisitely accurate. The pool, the swimming area, the little waterfall, the undulating knolls, the high ground, the field between the pool and the trees, and the trees were precisely portrayed in the sand. Ponce studied his renderings. Without drawing the fences and buildings, he visualized the map as it would appear after construction. Visions of his palace, the servants' quarters, the hanging gardens, the stables, a zoo featuring local wildlife, thick stone walls, and a magnificent entry gate staffed by uniformed guards played in his head. He would fill in every detail later. For now, he had to get there, secure it, and control it.

"The Indians say we have to camp in the open on the other side of this grove or down this canyon. Juarez, did you inspect the canyon?"

"No, but they told us it would be a difficult climb back up to the pool."

"Then I guess we'll have to camp out here to start," Ponce said as he drew an X in the sand on the far side of the grove.

"What do you mean, to start?" Juarez asked.

"We're going to build a walled city around the source of my water. Then we're going to bring in more forces to secure it. After that, we'll get the Indians to convert the wooden walls to stout stone walls."

"How do you plan to do that? We have three horses, thirty men, and no guns," Juarez asked.

With bravado, José said, "We have armor, long swords, battle tactics, and experience on our side."

"On the ship, we have cannons and more guns. We can send the ship for more men and supplies," Pedro said.

"Wait a minute. Why are you building a wall around the Vortex?"

"To secure and protect it."

"From what?"

"From heathens and anybody else we don't want there. Don't you understand, the source will be a retreat for royalty and popes. I will entertain them there—at the Fountain of Youth. It must be secure." Then Ponce turned to José and Pedro. "You are now doing God's work. Are you with me?"

"Do I understand that you are going to move this camp to that X and begin building a wall?" Juarez asked.

"Yes, of course."

"I think we should honor what Manchun told us."

"He'll come around. I will talk to him. When he understands, he will give us what we need."

"Until he agrees, I want you to tell me you'll honor your words."

"Of course, of course."

Juarez looked Ponce in the eyes. Ponce looked away and asked José how long it would take to build a timber fence around the Vortex. José told him it would depend on the number and types of trees available.

"There are plenty of trees in this grove," Ponce said as he poked his stick in the sand representation.

"Don't touch those trees until we have an agreement with Manchun," Juarez said.

"Okay, how long will it take to move this camp up there?" Ponce asked Pedro.

"If we use all three horses to pack supplies, we can prepare and move the day after tomorrow."

"Do it."

It pleased Pedro that Ponce had given him important responsibilities. He left the meeting and exerted his newfound authority unnecessarily, to pack and prepare for moving the camp. Likewise, José located axes and supplies that would help him build the compound walls. It pleased Ponce that the activity level picked up in camp. His men seemed pleased to have a definite mission. Juarez went to his tent very, very, very concerned. He could see a rising tide that he may not be able to control. He thought he would try to talk to Ponce in the morning after a good night's sleep.

At first light, Pedro urged the men under his control to prepare for the move. The early camp activity pleased Ponce; it motivated him even more. He strolled through the camp, pushing his men on. Juarez decided to wait before trying to talk to him. Instead, he bridled a horse and told Ponce he wanted to ride out and inspect the trails. He exited the camp, hoping Petnima or Gurefin would notice and meet him away from the camp. He assumed the Natives watched every move the Spaniards made and that his ride would provide access to them. When Juarez rounded a small hill, beyond sight of the encampment, Gurefin met him on the trail.

"Why are you out here alone?"

"I wanted to talk to you. Ponce is more obsessed than ever. I feared that if I tried to talk to him this morning he wouldn't listen. I want you to listen. The camp is moving tomorrow. Ponce has promised me that he would camp where Manchun directed and I will direct the men to respect the pools. I don't know what I will do if Ponce gets completely out of control. In a lot of ways, I'm glad you have the guns. Unfortunately, Ponce still commands me."

"Yes. It makes me feel good that you are trying to be reasonable without betraying your responsibilities," Gurefin said.

"I'm happy you can appreciate my position."

"Would Ponce be reasonable if we proved the water was just simple water?"

"That would be my hope. I suspect the stingray poison would have resolved with the hot compresses regardless of the water."

Gurefin nodded.

"I even believe the medicine for the poisonous plants had less to with water than other ingredients."

Again, Gurefin nodded. "I'll talk to Manchun to let him work on it. Together, maybe we can get through this without bloodshed."

"I'm going up the trail a little further; would you like to ride along?"

"I'd like to but I'm riding out to bring in some more people. Unfortunately, some of them are archers."

"I see. I hope you don't need them, but I understand your precautions."

Gurefin rode off, and Juarez rode up the trail alone. He now had very real concerns for everybody's safety. In his heart he knew the Natives would defend the Vortex and themselves, like any self-respecting people. But now it was cutting close to home and in real time. He worked on scenarios whereby he could bring Ponce to earth and retreat from his plans with respect.

After all, Gurefin had just conceded that the water was nothing more than water. But Juarez feared that Ponce would never release the fantasy. Water had been implanted in his psyche before he went to Granada. He had been seeking it throughout his career. In his mind, the Fountain of Youth fulfilled his quest for self-realization. His life's work had been achieved. How could anybody pull him off that mount? Juarez knew he had to work on it. He continued to ride and turned back only after he had reached the rocky mountainside. He juggled possible arguments to present to Ponce, but none seemed promising. He would have to let a conversation evolve. At one time, Ponce esteemed logic; perhaps he could point out logical fallacies when Ponce presented them. He would try.

By the time Juarez returned to the camp, Pedro had the camp well-organized, and the men looked forward to the move. Brief descriptions of the source ignited their imaginations. Juarez sought out Ponce and asked him to accompany him to the riverbank where they could talk.

"You know, Ponce, we've heard the comment 'things aren't always what they seem' from several sources. We've also been advised not to be disappointed when we reached the source. I think we should give some consideration to what we've been told."

"Now they're just trying to downplay the importance of the water," Ponce said. His quick reply implied no thought had gone into his response.

"Why would they do that?"

"So we won't settle there."

"You know that this river flows from the source, don't you?"

"It's not the same."

"How could it have changed?"

"Think about it. The pure water flows from the Fountain of Youth. To benefit from it you must take it from the source when it's fresh."

Juarez recognized a crack in Ponce's logic and built a logical response that he hoped would force Ponce to acknowledge it. "Does the quality of the water deteriorate once it leaves the source?"

"Yes, now you understand. It's obvious, the Fountain of Youth must be enshrined, and all believers must pay homage at the temple. Popes and kings will come to drink from the Fountain of Youth at the shrine we shall build."

Ponce had deflected the issue of fresh water. Juarez decided to drive the point home in more detail. "Will the popes and kings take jugs of water home with them? And if they do, will the water have the same qualities?"

"No, only water at the source is divine."

"Not divine, then, but will it have any healing powers?"

"It must be at the source," Ponce impatiently answered.

Juarez knew Ponce's attention had dwindled but he had to make his point. "If that were true, how do you account for the healing of the string ray attack, the poison plant irritations, or my snake bite?"

Ponce exploded, "You're a heretic, that's blasphemous! This conversation is over. And watch how you talk about my water."

Juarez watched Ponce stomp emphatically back into camp. Juarez turned back toward the river. He knew he was in trouble; all the Spaniards were in trouble. He also knew the innocent Natives could be in trouble. With no apparent discourse available, Juarez contemplated as many options as he could conjure.

Mutiny could prove a death sentence at both ends. José and Pedro could easily bring the rest of men with them to side with Ponce. If that didn't happen, Juarez knew he could face trials in Spain for arresting the governor of Florida. Mutiny wasn't an option. He had already warned the Natives without violating his responsibilities to the governor. If he went further with the Natives, he could be cited for insurrection. Unless he wanted to live with the Natives for the rest of his life, that wasn't an option.

Perhaps he could talk to José and Pedro to prevent them from following Ponce blindly into some serious blunders. That might be his best option, he thought. Whether they listened to him or not, he would move with the camp and try to maintain the peace.

Juarez caught up to José late in the afternoon. "Do you have everything you need to build the fences?" he asked.

"I have two axes, a hatchet, a wedge, and a heavy hammer. I wish I had more. There are more on the ship."

"I don't think we're going back there soon. Have you ever built a log wall before?"

"I helped with a small wall on Hispaniola."

"Did you have to read instructions there?" Juarez asked.

"I can't read or write. I pay attention and work hard."

"Okay. Be sure we don't get ahead of ourselves up there." That interaction didn't encourage Juarez. José came to take orders and fight when asked. He wasn't likely to listen to reason.

Later in the evening, just before dark, Juarez helped Pedro wrap and tie a bundle of munitions. "We want to take care of this one."

"Until we get the guns back, we won't need it."

"You never know. You've done a good job getting ready for the move. How did you happen to come on this expedition?"

"My dad was a sailor on ships to the east and I grew up around the docks."

"Did you go to school there?"

"There was no school. It was a rough life. One of Columbus's men saw how I could fight and asked me to sail with them. That got me to Puerto Rico where I helped fight the Indians. Ponce noticed me and looked me up for this expedition."

Pedro wasn't going to be the enlightened one either. Juarez felt isolated.

After a fitful night, Juarez watched as the camp remnants were packed on the horses, the men hefted loads on their backs, and Ponce led the procession north toward the source. Even with his determination, Ponce on foot would make this a long day. Juarez took a position on a large rock and watched the men proceed. When they had passed, he followed them up the trail.

Targonsa and five riders with long bows paced the caravan, staying mostly out of sight. Manchun, Gurefin, and Petnima rode straight to the Vortex to advise their friends and the additional archers. The archers kept three types of arrows in their arsenal: normal flint-tipped arrows, poison arrows, and pitch-based arrows for sending fireballs into the enemy. Many of the archers also rode well. Targonsa and his companions watched the Spaniards march stoically up the trail until they reached the steep mountainside. Ponce, who was drenched in a heavy sweat, led the procession up the mountainside one painful step after another. Targonsa almost felt sorry for them.

By early afternoon, Ponce had achieved the summit. He looked out over the long grassy plateau toward the grove of oak trees in the far distance. He called a halt and gave his men a rest and an opportunity to look out over what he considered his promised land. Finally, all the men attained the summit, and the destination revealed itself to them as they committed themselves to finishing the heavy and clumsy trek. Ponce's intoxicated anticipation pushed him on.

CHAPTER 12

Well before dark, the men unloaded, unpacked, and began to build an orderly camp. Ponce went to his tent and napped. Juarez called a meeting to lay out the rules for the area. Bathing and laundry should be done in small groups at the lower end of the small pool at the waterfall early in the mornings. Do not disturb the Natives. Respect all living things. He led two men with jugs to collect water for the camp.

In the morning, Ponce, Juarez, and five men went to the pool to bathe. When they returned, eight more men headed for the pool. Ponce and Juarez walked through the camp, checking the men and the bathing schedule. The grooms had water for the horses and had harvested enough grass to keep them happy. Ponce said he wanted to ride his horse to the pool.

"I don't think that would be acceptable. You don't want to disrespect the Natives or what you agreed to do with Manchun."

"Do you think he would judge me on that?"

"I think everything we do is being judged. You don't see them riding horses over there. Let's try to behave like the Natives when we're over there."

"Maybe you're right, for now. I'll take a walk around."

Ponce left Juarez in camp and walked through the oak trees, across the grassy field, and to the Vortex. He walked slowly and remained alert for a visit from Manchun. An elderly Native made his way slowly onto a low knoll where he sat and watched the water. Ponce wondered why he had come here to do nothing more than sit. "Why would he object if I built a wall?" he asked himself. A young boy and girl walked to the old man and sat with him. They spoke in low tones and showed respect for each other. Ponce failed to recognize any value in that interaction either.

He continued his watch for Manchun. He made himself available at the Vortex for over an hour before he left and walked through the oak grove. Ponce stopped at an immense oak tree with a circumference, at the base, of at least twelve feet. Congruous with his mental state, he wanted the world to know that this tree too, belonged to him. He would order José to use his axe to carve his name into the bark after he etched the letters for him.

Manchun and Gurefin rode their horses at a long distance from the Spanish camp to determine appropriate observation posts and closer-range access trails. They returned and visited many small camps with their friends to inform them of some of the best means to monitor the Spanish activities. Observers stationed themselves in the oak grove, along the trail to the lower pool, and in the grasslands. Targonsa and his riding archers rode through the grasslands at a greater distance with their long bows. That night, an observer from the oak grove reported to Manchun that a Spaniard had been cutting bark off one of the largest trees.

"What do you think, Gurefin?" Manchun asked.

"Did it appear likely that he wanted to cut the tree down?"

"I don't think so. He was just marking it."

"We can't let them take liberties here. They must respect it," Gurefin said.

"Okay, show me the tree in the morning; we'll try to find Ponce," Manchun said.

Early in the morning, Manchun and the observer walked into the grove. A mist circulated in the highest tree branches. The morning moisture and limited light created a peaceful setting. Manchun and his observer walked slowly and quietly, appreciating the quality of the scene. Wood chips littering the ground around the large tree appeared out of place but would blend back into the forest, eventually. The carvings on the tree told a different story. This tree would be disfigured for a long time. Manchun agreed that this activity couldn't be allowed. They walked through the grove toward the Spanish camp.

Manchun contacted a guard and asked for a word with Ponce. The guard sent a messenger for Ponce. "Good morning. I'm glad to see you, I want to tell you how important this place is to me."

"It has always been important to us, and that's why I came to you today. We always respect everything here and we expect our guests to do the same." Manchun attempted to allow Ponce to consider himself a guest.

"We'll take care of it," Ponce said.

"Why did you cut the bark from the big tree, then?"

"It won't hurt the tree."

Manchun realized that his words had little effect on Ponce. "We consider it defiling the tree and consequently, defiling the area—the Vortex."

Ponce looked a bit perplexed. He couldn't imagine anybody would ever care about him cutting his name into a tree. It wouldn't hurt anybody, and the tree would live. "If that's important to you, okay."

"It is."

Ponce nodded after he considered further engagement. He decided that pushing for any concession would be better served later. He walked back into camp, pondering the situation. How could he make a breakthrough? Without horses and guns, his best efforts would be severely compromised. Even long swords wielded by experienced warriors would be a weak match against archers on horseback. Either he would have to get the horses and guns back or he would have to cajole Manchun into leaving the area peaceably. He went to Juarez and asked how they could get the guns and horses back.

"I don't think we're getting them back. It's not like we put them on loan for a week."

"What do we have that they would trade for?"

"Nothing. They have everything they need. They don't want stuff."

"Okay. When do you think they'll go away and leave us alone here?"

"Never. They've been coming here for a long time. There's no reason for them to quit this beautiful place. It's especially important to them."

"You're not encouraging."

"I'm trying to be a good soldier and tell you the truth. That's the only way I can be loyal to you."

"Well, while you're trying to be loyal, find a way to secure this area."

"I'll let you know if I hear anything from the Natives."

"You do that." Ponce walked away, talking to himself. He liked loyalty; he would like it a lot more if everybody would join him in pursuing his personal quest. For the rest of the day, he walked through the camp and ordered his men to assure that their battle gear was in good condition.

Late in the afternoon, he summoned two divers to his tent. "I want you to casually walk to the source and watch for any Indians diving or swimming at the deep end, under that rock face. Don't disturb anybody, and be respectful. Go there in the morning and report back to me tomorrow afternoon."

The divers went to the pool as appointed; they watched and waited. About midday, two young girls swam into the deep end from the shallow end. They touched the rock face and swam back. Other than that, it had been a peaceful but boring assignment. As they thought about leaving, a young man climbed onto the rock face and made the twenty-foot dive into the clear water. He surfaced, climbed back up the rock, and tried to perfect his technique. After his second dive, he swam to the low end of the pool. The divers watched for another hour with no activity in the water before they returned to camp. They went to Ponce and told him about the two girls and the diver.

Ponce asked excitedly about the diver. "Did he dive deep down to the cave entrance?"

"It didn't look like he swam down any deeper than the dive took him."

"Could he have been looking for something down there?"

"The water is so clear, he could see anything down there without diving."

Ponce let his unsubstantiated thoughts escape. "It must be in the cave."

"What about a cave?"

"There's a cave down there. I think they're hiding something in it. I want you to take José with you tomorrow and dive down to the cave and see what you can find."

The divers couldn't think of a better way to spend the day than diving and swimming in clear cool water. They could see one drawback. "We'll do that, but José isn't much of a swimmer."

"He doesn't have to dive, just take him with you to watch while you dive."

José and the divers returned to the Vortex in the morning. "Let's swim around first, before we go deep off the rock."

José seated himself on the rock and watched the swimmers. They surfaced and climbed up the rock. They told José they could see a possible cave entrance, but it appeared deep. One diver dove deep and close to the cave entrance. He surfaced and said there was a definite cave, but he didn't have enough air to explore it. He said he could do it if he planned it better. The second diver said he would follow him down on the second dive. They did some deep breathing and prepared to dive. They went into the clear water one after another. José watched them swim toward where they said the entrance broke into the rock wall. They disappeared into the entrance almost together. José watched intently for their reappearance. Suddenly José became concerned. Then he felt terrified. They had been down for over a minute. He knew he couldn't hold his breath that long, but they were good divers, they could do it. He continued to watch. They didn't come out from the entrance. For minutes he watched without any idea of what to do. Then he thought; surely there was another exit. That's it; they swam out in another part of the pool. He began his search. He ran all the way around the pool—no divers. Then he panicked and ran across the field and continued to run through the grove and into the camp. He went to Ponce's tent and interrupted a conversation with Juarez. "The divers are lost," he said, as he gasped for breath.

"What? Lost! Where did they go?"

"They dove and swan into the . . . the cave, but they never came out." José tried to catch his breath. "They never came out. I ran all the way around the pool to find another exit but couldn't find them. They're gone."

"Why were they diving into the cave?" Juarez asked.

"I sent them," Ponce said.

"You what? Manchun told you there was a current there."

"There's something in that cave."

"Yeah, two of our men."

"Leave me alone. Both of you."

Gurefin, Petnima, and Manchun listened attentively to the report of the divers' plight.

"They entered the cave. They're gone. What did the third Spaniard do?" Manchun asked.

"He ran around the pool searching for them. Then he ran all the way back to camp."

"I wonder what they'll do about that. You told them to stay away from the cave," Gurefin said.

"They're hard to convince."

"I can't imagine what they'll try next," Manchun said.

"I can try to talk to Juarez," Petnima said.

"He can't violate his responsibilities," Gurefin said.

"I wouldn't expect him to do that, but he may offer a no answer or a smile."

"Well if you want to do that, be careful," Manchun said.

In the morning, Juarez needed some time alone. He took his horse and rode south in the big field to the overlook Petnima had shown him on their first trip. As he rode, he worried about Ponce's hopeless desperation. How could he reason with him before that desperate man committed desperate deeds?

At the overlook, Juarez hobbled his horse and found a perch. He set about contemplating Ponce's lifestyle, wants, needs, and desires, which coincided with his until recently. He contrasted that with the Natives' peaceful coexistence with nature. Unintentionally, his mind drifted back to his childhood. His father gathered enough from the sea to survive. His family had little, but they were happy. Somehow as a young man he didn't appreciate that, and he began his quest for more. The need for stuff provided an easy contrast.

How about conquest? They had come here to conquer and control as much of the new world as possible. What are the Natives' territorial bounds? Are they attempting to expand to new territories? Do they face threats from their neighbors? He knew they would fight to defend this territory. He could easily visualize himself squarely in the middle of an unfortunate battle.

He managed a short nap before he went to his horse and gave her an extensive rub down, as if she were his only friend on earth. He considered Petnima, Gurefin, Manchun, and Targonsa as friendly, but he was not one them. Maybe his horse was his only friend. He climbed aboard and let his horse carry him gently through the tall grasses toward the steep mountain. He gave the horse the lead and closed his eyes. He felt every careful footstep, which foot was up, which was down. He simply wished something would change.

At the steep mountain, he turned around and headed home. By the time he entered the camp, nothing had changed, except that the guard told him that Indian woman came by and asked about him. He had missed her visit, and that didn't help his disposition. He asked the cook for something to eat and walked through the trees to the pool.

At the pool, his daily fortunes changed. Petnima called to him and met him at the water. "A guard said you had asked for me."

"Yes, I wanted to ask if you'd like to ride up into some new territory tomorrow."

"I really would. I don't seem to be getting much accomplished here."

"Good, I'll meet you on the other side of the trees in the morning."

"I'll be ready."

Juarez told Ponce he'd be gone for the day. Ponce waved goodbye to him. Ponce wanted some negotiation movement. A quick thought provided a path he wanted to explore. Without Juarez's negative attitude, perhaps he could force some changes in the Indians' mindset. Juarez had convinced him that an all-out battle plan could be a disaster. So far, peaceful negotiations had been deflected. He thought perhaps some combination of strength and negotiation could resolve some of his frustration. He called for Pedro and José. He told them to have the men remain in camp and be prepared for his orders.

As planned, Petnima met Juarez by the trees and they rode north at a gallop for a short distance just to escape the camp atmosphere.

With the horses at a walk they continued, mostly in silence, until they reached a pine forest.

"This is a soft and quiet place with the pine needles on the ground. I hope the horses like it," Petnima said.

"I like it. I need to be away from the camp. I see problems brewing and I can't find a way to slow them down. I fear my companions will destroy your peace."

"We're concerned too. We've tried to prepare for our defense, but it's so uncertain. We're not innocent in building these tensions, you know."

"How's that?"

"We lied to you about the water. It has no magical power. You were correct in believing that hot compresses alone relieved the pain from the stingray. Only when the barb breaks off under the skin is it a serious problem. You were also correct about the potion for the poisonous plants."

"But how did I survive the snake bite?"

"If you had paid close attention you would have noticed that the three-colored snake that killed your companion had colored bands situated so that yellow bands touched the red bands. The snake you encountered had bands situated such that yellow bands touched the black bands, not the red bands."

"There had to be a logical answer."

"I'm sorry. You were so gullible that we found any reason to allow you to believe the misinformation. I'm not proud of it."

Juarez laughed and said, "I would have found it difficult to give up a good hoax. All of you made it appear so real." He continued to laugh. After a few seconds, he stopped and thought about it. Then he began to laugh even harder.

"You're laughing. Do you think it's funny?"

"I'm not afraid to laugh at myself. Like I appreciate good horsemanship, I can appreciate a good joke, even if it's on me. But . . . I'm going to have a word with Manchun. He scraped the skin off my arm and hit my arm with that rock. Then we'll have another good laugh together."

"The problem is that we thought you would go back after you discovered that the source is nothing more than water."

"There's more to it than you can realize. It's a perfect conflagration. Let me give you the story in its entirety. Ponce, as a young man, was blessed by a holy man. He was told that water was his destiny. By itself that doesn't mean anything, but in that culture, it's an invitation to chase a dream. You see, there is a belief that somewhere in the world there exists a Fountain of Youth. Great expeditions have sought it. With the discovery of this new world, rumors circulated promulgating that the Fountain of Youth would be found here. The king of Spain gave him permission to explore all these lands and to find the Fountain of Youth. Do you see the problem?"

Petnima's eyes opened wide and she gasped, "Oh my, yes. When we gave the water magical qualities . . . Ponce knew he had found it."

"He still believes it. I tried to explain it to him. He said I was crazy. It's his quest and I don't know how he will ever give it up. He believes it. He believes his god put him here to secure it. It goes beyond human reason."

"That puts a more serious tone on it. What will we do? My people will never give up the Vortex."

"I would never expect them to do that," Juarez said.

"If weapons get exposed by both sides, something terrible could happen."

"That's what I've been worrying about."

Although concerned about misinterpretations and the possibility of hostilities, Petnima and Juarez rode through the tranquil pine forest relishing the ability to share mutual concerns. That was something

Juarez couldn't do with anybody in the Spanish camp. Juarez was thankful for the moment.

Meanwhile, back at the camp, Ponce, with no stabilizing influence available to oppose him, fixated on forcing some movement toward securing the source. He sent a guard out to find an Indian to request a meeting with Manchun. The guard walked along the tree line until one of Targonsa's riders called to him. The guard raised his hand and walked toward the rider. Within a loud talking distance, he informed the rider that Ponce wanted a meeting with Manchun at the edge of the camp. The rider said he would pass the message on and rode off. The rider found Manchun with Targonsa and Gurefin. He relayed the request and waited on his horse.

"What do you think he wants now? Why doesn't he just go away?" Gurefin said.

"He's not likely to get anything more from us. He's making me tired."

"Do you want to meet with him?"

"No, but maybe I should go. Unfortunately, the voice of reason is out riding with Petnima," Manchun said.

"We'll go with you," Gurefin said. Then he told the rider to ride back and tell the Spaniards they would meet soon. He also ordered him to put everybody on alert but to stay out of sight. The archers and the mounted patrol understood their responsibilities.

Manchun walked with Targonsa and Gurefin to the camp and found Ponce forward of twenty-some men, with Pedro and José at his side. Gurefin whispered, "I don't like this."

"He's serious today. Follow my lead," Manchun whispered back.

"Do you understand how important that water is to me?" Ponce asked in a strong and positive voice.

"It's just water, but this area is the most important thing to us," Manchun answered.

"You can't understand that this source is something the people in the old world have sought for centuries."

"How do you know this is the spot and how could your people across the sea know it's here?"

"I know it's here. I've seen what the water can do."

"Well let's stop shouting about it." Then Manchun told Gurefin and Targonsa to stay put as he walked to be face-to-face with Ponce. "The magic you've seen has all been contrived. Things are seldom what they seem."

"That's nonsense. The water saved my diver from the stingray poison."

"No. The water had nothing to do with it. Hot compresses drew the poison out."

"I don't believe it. We need another stingray to prove that."

"There are no stingrays here."

The veins on Ponce's neck began to swell. "What about the relief from the poisonous plants?" Ponce asked in a demanding way. What he demanded was the answer he wanted to hear.

Manchun couldn't help him out. "Again, we fooled you. The medication that relieves the discomfort from poisonous plants comes from the inner bark of a special tree and some local plants. Any water helps us spread it over the affected area."

"We're not fools. We've seen it work." Ponce's answer confirmed that he wasn't listening to the explanations. He was on the verge of being out of control. Pedro and José stood by their leader. Some of the men behind them had puzzled looks on their faces.

"You don't know this part of the world. I can take you to more clear-water pools like this within easy two-day rides. There is nothing different about the water at those pools than at this one."

"Why did you bring us here?"

"This is the closest pool to your settlement. We wanted to explain and apologize for our mischievous behavior in a place where we could all relax and enjoy the beauty."

"I don't believe you. You're trying to get us to go back. I'm not going back."

"I think we should leave. You're not listening."

Ponce almost shouted, "Then what about saving Juarez from the three-colored snake?"

Manchun backed one step and produced a small smile. "There are two kinds of three-colored snakes."

"You're lying. You're all liars. When are you going to give us the horses and guns back?" Ponce's voice cracked as he shouted the question.

"We're not," Manchun said softly but emphatically.

Ponce clenched his fists. Then he pounded one fist into his other hand. He stomped his foot and issued a shrill screech. "Grab him and hold him," Ponce shouted. Pedro and José each took a strong grip on Manchun's arms and turned him around so that he faced Gurefin and Targonsa, who watched from twenty feet away.

"Shall we release the archers?" Targonsa asked.

"Hold on—let's try to save Manchun," Gurefin said.

Ponce drew his long sword and held it high, pointed skyward. His arm holding the sword shook uncontrollably. "I'm claiming this entire area for the king of Spain and the pope," Ponce shouted. Then he drew a knife with his left hand and held it out to show it to Targonsa and Gurefin. "Now tell them to return the guns and bring me the horses or I will use this knife." Manchun remained silent. Ponce continued to shake the sword high in the air. "Tell them now!" Ponce's voice was loud, hoarse, and hysterical.

Manchun spoke softly and without apparent fear. "You can kill me now, but it will be sure death for you and all of your men. Have you not seen our archers in the trees and around your camp?"

"You're still lying! Bring me my horses and guns!" Ponce desperately screamed.

Manchun shouted, "You have your orders!" Gurefin issued a shrill whistle and archers stepped into the open from behind trees and tall grasses. Riders on horseback began to circle the camp.

Ponce panicked and exploded into action. He stabbed at Manchun's back and brought his sword's handle down hard on Manchun's head. Manchun collapsed in the grass. Ponce raised his bloody left hand and knife, then Pedro, José, and Ponce backstepped toward the Spaniards aligned behind them, to no avail. A rain of arrows fell upon the Spaniards. Pedro and José took fatal hits, and another arrow incapacitated Ponce when it hit him in the upper thigh. Four additional Spaniards were wounded. The remaining Spaniards huddled together and backed slowly toward their camp. The next round brought fire arrows that landed on the tents, which began to burn. The Spaniards huddled together with their swords, machetes, and knives. Without leadership, they positioned themselves back to back and waited. Gurefin ordered the archers to circle the Spaniards and shoot any of them that attempted to leave the group. The horse patrol rode slowly around the Spaniards, ready to control anyone trying to escape.

Petnima and Juarez rode on, beginning to reveal stories of their personal lives, until—"Thunder? It can't be thunder. There's not a cloud in the sky."

"Oh no. It must have been a gunpowder explosion. We must get back. What has Ponce done?"

Petnima stared at Juarez with a terrified look. "Let's go." They rode at a gallop back through the pine trees. When the horses had had enough, they walked them and worried silently. From the tall grass field, they watched flames from the Spanish camp. Now the horses had to be pushed again. They rode straight through the horse patrol and archers to Manchun in the grass.

"What happened?" Juarez shouted. None of the Spaniards answered. He pointed to a single Spaniard and ordered him to come to him. "I asked you what happened."

"Ponce killed him because he wouldn't return the horses."

"Is he dead?"

"No, but he's losing a lot of blood."

Juarez called to Gurefin, "Get him into the trees and help him." Then he turned to the Spaniards still huddled and holding knives, machetes, and swords limply. They had no leader, no shelter, and no place to hide. "Drop your weapons and move away from them or you'll catch another round of arrows."

The Spaniards followed that order. Then Juarez noticed Ponce trying to crawl toward the rest of the men. "Why did you do this?"

"They're liars, liars, all liars. They don't respect my water, it's my water, my water." Ponce had obviously crossed over from reality.

"Do you want me to pull that arrow from your leg?"

"Yes. Then give the order to fight on. We must secure the water."

"The fight is over." Juarez called for two men to come take care of Ponce after he pulled the arrow out of his leg. He repeated his order to stay away from the weapons. He told the Natives to watch the men and keep them from the weapons. Then he went to the trees to attempt a temporary peace treaty. He carried the arrow he pulled from Ponce.

"Don't touch the end of that arrow," Petnima said.

"I pulled it from Ponce's leg."

"He's a dead man. It'll be slow, but almost certainly a dead man," Gurefin said.

Juarez held the arrow away from him with a quizzical look.

"See the red band near the feathers? It was a poison arrow."

"He's out of his head right now. Your men have our men surrounded and away from their weapons," Juarez said.

"We'll have to figure out what to do with them," Gurefin said.

"How is Manchun?"

"He'll live. Ponce tried to stab him in the back, but his knife hit the shoulder blade and was deflected. There's no internal damage. There'll be a big scar," Targonsa said.

"I can live with that," Manchun whispered as he opened his eyes.

"Were there any other injuries?" Juarez asked.

"I don't think so. They didn't have any way to deliver any blows."

"Good. With your permission, I'll have my men dig graves for the dead men out there. Then our fate is up to you. I suggest you collect all the weapons in that pile," Juarez said.

Gurefin asked his men to go out to collect the weapons, and Juarez returned to his men and ordered a detail to dig graves.

Everyone had rejoiced when Manchun opened his eyes and spoke. Gurefin asked if he felt strong enough to discuss the situation.

"Is it necessary to take action now?"

"No, not until they bury the dead men. Then we'll make some decisions and post guards. I think they lost everything in the fire and explosion. They'll need food too," Gurefin said.

"Did I understand that Ponce took a poison arrow?"

"He did."

"He won't be a threat. How about the two men who were with him?"

"They're dead."

"Petnima, how was Juarez's attitude today?"

"He was afraid something like this would happen. He didn't expect it today. He explained why Ponce has been obsessed with the water. He had not been able to reason with him."

"I feel bad for Juarez. He's been stuck in a hard place. Targonsa, did you get the horses out of the camp okay?" Gurefin asked.

"We have them safe now."

"Let's get something cooked up for the Spaniards. When Juarez is available, I'd like to talk to him," Manchun said.

Juarez supervised the funeral proceedings then inspected the camp remnants. Almost everything lay in ruin. Very few material goods remained that would aid them on the long walk back to the settlement. He told the men to stay away from the camp and that he would go beg for some water and something to eat. Targonsa rode his horse to Juarez and asked if he'd come talk to Manchun.

CHAPTER 13

Juarez walked slowly to Manchun's small circle. "Come sit. I'm sorry I don't think I can stand right now," Manchun said.

"How are you? I heard them say you had no internal injuries."

"I think that's right. I'm looking forward to a complete recovery, in time."

"I can't tell you how sorry I am that this happened."

"Petnima told us how Ponce came to believe he was a world hero by discovering the Fountain of Youth. We weren't completely innocent either. I accept some responsibility for this. Also, I want you to know that I don't hold you responsible," Manchun said.

"Thank you for saying that. Now I'm responsible for those men out there and I don't know what my fate will be if Ponce lives long enough to file a report. What do you want to do with us?"

"Let's work together to get you back to the settlement. After that . . . maybe the ship should take you away."

"Those men don't belong here. We should leave," Juarez said.

"I won't be traveling for a while but Gurefin will work with you at the settlement. We are cooking now and will deliver food to the men shortly. Perhaps you should take them to the pool for water now," Manchun said.

"Gurefin, if we start the march back to the settlement in the morning, will you work with me to feed them along the way?"

"Yes, we'll make it as painless as possible. We don't hate anybody out there. We do think they should leave, though."

"Thank you." Juarez stood, and as he moved away from the circle, he noticed tears in Petnima's eyes. He tried not to acknowledge that.

Juarez met his men and told them the Natives would be bringing food for them and suggested that they all go to the pool for water. He also told them to fill any containers they could find. Two men lifted Ponce and helped him to the pool. At the pool, he refused to speak. He looked at the water, drank, and held his head in his hands.

Since the camp had been destroyed, at least they wouldn't be carrying armor, weapons, or tents on the trek back.

In the morning, Juarez prepared the men for the march back. Two men supported Ponce and they all followed Juarez toward the steep mountain. Targonsa's horse patrol rode along with the men. Many other Natives followed. Gurefin and Petnima followed the procession on their horses. The pace necessarily dragged due to Ponce's injury, as he painfully limped along with the aid of two men. An hour into the march, Petnima told Gurefin she could speed things up. Gurefin told her to fix it. She commandeered two horses and led them to the front of the pack.

"Juarez, you're now the leader and you should have a horse. Take this one. If you put Ponce up on the other one, life will be better for everyone," Petnima said.

Juarez looked up to her, said thank you, and climbed aboard. The two men carrying Ponce hefted him onto the horse and thanked her as well. Ponce remained silent, without acknowledging the help. Riding didn't relieve the pain in Ponce's leg. The wound had stopped bleeding, but it was tender, raw, and didn't look like he thought it should. He followed Juarez and contemplated how he would regain control. He was the governor and he could make life-and-death decisions. He wondered if he would find it necessary to make a call against Juarez.

Midafternoon, Ponce rode up next to Juarez. "How are we going to regain control when we're back at the settlement?"

Juarez decided to play it easy. "I don't know how to do that without any weapons."

"Well, how are we going to get our weapons back?"

"I don't think the Natives are going to give them back."

"How about the weapons at the settlement?"

"The Natives will take them first."

"We've got a ship full of guns with cannons."

"If we make it to the ship, we'll see what happens." The thought that Ponce would try to punish the Natives worried Juarez.

They marched until almost dark. The Natives distributed food and made water available. Juarez watched Ponce talk to two men quietly. He couldn't afford any insurrection on this trek. It could be a death sentence. Juarez called the two men to him for a short walk in the morning.

"I noticed you talking with Ponce last night. How is he doing?" Juarez asked.

"I don't think he's quite right anymore. Who's in charge now?"

"I am. I took control when Ponce was defeated and wounded. What did Ponce want?"

"He wanted us to sneak into the settlement and hide the guns before the Natives could get them. He also said we had them outnumbered."

Juarez debated whether to subtly implicate the men with the fact that they said Ponce wasn't right, or if he should put the fear of God in them. He decided that these men may not be able to comprehend their own implications. He decided on the latter. "I think we've proved to the Natives that we can't be trusted. If you are seen away from this group, you could catch an arrow and it could be a poison arrow like Ponce got. I would be careful. Come to me if Ponce talks about trying to fight."

"Do we have them outnumbered?"

"Not even close. You can see the archers on the horses. There are archers behind most of the trees and bushes all along this trail. Our only chance is to not give them a reason to start shooting at us." Juarez hoped the men would spread the warning.

The second day on the trail started as the last one ended. Ponce rode alone and in pain. Petnima wanted to ride up to Juarez and be with him. She thought better of it. He had to show his men he controlled the march and ensured their safety. She could disrupt their trust if she interfered. Petnima hoped she would have another opportunity to talk to him.

Juarez occasionally rode out to Gurefin or Targonsa to talk about how to secure the camp, and more important, to organize a strategy once they reached the settlement. If they made good progress today, they could be at the settlement the next day. Juarez told Gurefin that Ponce, although weak, tried to get two men to sneak into the settlement to secure the weapons. Gurefin asked Juarez if he could get the men in the settlement to surrender their weapons.

"I'll try. If it works, we'll have to search the entire settlement before we allow anybody in there. Maybe we should move immediately onto the ship and leave everything," Juarez said.

"See how you feel about that when we get there. How does the wound in Ponce's leg look?"

"It's not responding like I would expect."

"That's normal. I don't know how you feel about it, but he will die from the wound. The poison he received prevents the wound from healing. He will grow weaker until he dies."

"If I can keep the men from taking up his cause, we'll be okay. I think the men have had enough of his obsession with the water."

The trek halted a short time before sunset and Targonsa brought another meal in for the men. They had traversed a lot of territory in two days, and some of the men recognized that they would almost certainly arrive at the settlement the next day. Gurefin met Juarez in the camp area and asked if any of the men required any special attention. Juarez gave all the men an opportunity to ask for help. None of the men asked for anything.

Ponce attempted to stand and address the men. His words were jumbled and the pain in his leg forced him to sit without making any point the men could comprehend. Juarez thought that, as unfortunate as Ponce's condition was, his incoherent speech served a purpose. The men would be less inclined to follow any orders he issued. Petnima rode her horse around the small circle. Juarez smiled and waved to her but didn't leave the men.

Petnima watched the sunset and sought a solution that would allow her to be with Juarez. She wondered how she could ever go to Spain with him. Castles, gold, greed, kings, and popes made that option particularly unappealing. Could she be with him on one of the islands in the new world? She recollected what she had heard about how the Spaniards had treated the Natives on the islands. That was even less appealing. Could he ever give up his stuff and stay here with her? That's what she wanted but soon realized that it would be as threatening to him as her going to Spain. There were no easy answers. She settled on a positive and honest farewell when it had to happen.

In the morning, word spread through the camp that they would be back to the settlement late in the afternoon. That gave everybody the energy to proceed without complaint. Gurefin shared Juarez's option of putting his men on the ship and sailing as soon as they reached the beach. That worried Petnima. She hoped that didn't happen.

With only two hours of marching to reach the beach, Juarez named two men to take charge of the other men, then rode out to meet with Gurefin, Targonsa, and Petnima. He recommended that Gurefin and three or four other riders accompany him to the settlement ahead of the procession. They could ascertain the situation there and attempt to disarm the men. Gurefin agreed and selected four of his riders to ride ahead with them.

The advance party rode onto the beach and noted that the ship still rocked peacefully in the bay. Nobody from the settlement noticed them. They rode to the settlement gate and Juarez called out. Two men ran to the gate. "Yes sir."

"Where is everybody?"

"Three men are working in the garden, and we have the captain and four men on the ship."

"Ponce has a serious injury and the rest of the men will arrive soon. Is there water on the ship?"

"Our standing orders were to keep the ship fully stocked. There is water and plenty of food on board."

"Good job. Will you call the other men and meet us here on the beach?"

"Yes sir."

Five unarmed men exited the compound gates and walked to Juarez and the Natives on horseback. "How many guns do you have in the compound?"

"We each have a gun here. You took the rest of them."

"Okay. Two of you go back and collect the guns. Bring them out and put them over there on the sand."

Two men obeyed without questioning Juarez. They carefully placed the guns on a clump of salt grass away from the settlement gate. The men returned to Juarez.

"Men, we've had a problem. Ponce tried to kill our friend Manchun. Some of our men are dead. The Natives have the horses and our guns. They are treating us well, but we will have to leave. Please stay out of the settlement and away from the guns. If we don't object to those orders, they will treat us well. Now, I want you to prepare the longboat to transport the men to the ship when they arrive." The men retrieved the longboat from up the beach and positioned it near the surf. Gurefin instructed one rider to position himself near the guns. He smiled at Juarez, recognizing that it appeared the violence would not resume.

Juarez rode down the beach with Gurefin. "I have one more fear. The ship has cannons—big guns—they can fire at you on the beach. I'm going to tell these men that if the captain fires even one shot, you will rain fire arrows onto the ship. These men haven't seen your fire arrows, but the other men know how they work and how they destroyed the camp. Have your riders perform like good actors and help me convince everyone that our lives are in danger when I transport the men back to the ship."

"We can be good actors. I am going to miss you. But we know you must go."

"I will miss you as well. I wish you peace. There is one thing I want to retrieve from the settlement. Is it okay?"

"You know I trust you. You do whatever you want."

Juarez gave Gurefin the reins to his horse and walked into the settlement to his cabin and brought a leather case onto the beach. "This is a chronicle of our activities here since we first arrived on the beach." He dropped it in the sand ten yards from the longboat. Then he walked to the five men waiting patiently. In a serious voice that the men accepted as fear based, Juarez explained that the Natives had fire arrows and that they had used them to destroy the camp at the Vortex. He said he was repeating a warning the Natives had given him. If the ship fired even one shot, the Natives would burn the ship and kill everybody in the water. He also made up a story that led the men to believe that although most of the Natives meant them no harm, some of the archers would kill them if they didn't move fast enough and obey all orders. Juarez left them to stew on that news, returned to Gurefin, and remounted his horse.

Fifteen minutes later, Ponce rode onto the beach, followed by his band of weary warriors. Juarez rode to Ponce and took the reins from him. He led his horse to the longboat and dismounted. He went to two men and ordered them to get Ponce on the ship and into the captain's cabin. He further instructed them to stay with him there until the ship sailed. Then he told them to help Ponce off the horse and get in the longboat with him.

In rapid succession he issued orders as if time were running out. He selected the four men with minor upper body wounds to make the first ride to the ship. He selected four more men to work the oars. With Ponce in the longboat, he ordered the oarsmen to launch the longboat, then the four wounded men waded into the surf and climbed aboard. He told three of the men from the settlement to join them on the first trip. Juarez waded into the surf and helped push the boat through the surf. He shouted to the men he selected from the settlement to tell the captain about the fire arrows and that the captain had to prepare to sail immediately.

Juarez watched the longboat speed toward the ship. Carefully and quickly, the longboat was tied to the ship and the men climbed up the ladder. When the last man climbed over the gunwale, the longboat started back to the beach. Juarez critically watched the activity on board. He wanted to see a sense of urgency. Three men shouted to the captain about the situation and the warnings. The captain came on deck and shouted at the longboat, then he began issuing orders to get men to the anchor capstan and into the rigging. That pleased Juarez.

When the longboat landed on the beach, an oarsman said the captain wanted to know what Ponce's problem was. Juarez sent ten more men into the longboat and waded into the surf to help the oarsmen work through the surf. Again, the longboat was tied to the ship and men scrambled up the ladder. While the longboat powered toward the beach, Juarez shouted that time was running out. The urgency in his voice kept the men on edge.

Gurefin, Targonsa, and Petnima watched the frenetic activity on the beach and onboard the ship. "He's got the fear in them he wanted," Gurefin said. He then told his riders to ride wildly around the beach. That would add to the urgency and confusion.

"I don't want him to leave. What's the big hurry?" Petnima asked.

"If he can convince them that their death is imminent, he can control them. If he can do that, we can avoid violence. It's working."

The longboat landed on the beach and Juarez shouted for the remaining men to turn it around before they climbed in. He told the men he feared some of the Natives could start shooting arrows at any time. He ran up the beach to a Native archer.

"Will you give me one arrow, please?"

The archer handed him an arrow. He ran back to the longboat and began to push it into the surf. The longboat was almost afloat. Then he stopped. "I've got to get my bag. Try to get started. I'll run and jump in," he shouted.

He ran toward his bag on the beach. He stumbled and crumpled face first in the sand. Feathers from an arrow pointed skyward from his motionless body.

"They shot him in the back," a passenger from the longboat shouted.

"We must get him," another man said.

"He's dead. Let's go." The lifeless body would serve no purpose in the longboat. Reality set in. If they didn't row now, they could catch the next round of arrows. The oarsmen pulled hard and the longboat lifted off the sand. The oarsmen considered their lives at risk. They rowed harder than ever. Juarez remained alone and motionless on the beach. The longboat reached the ship and the men scrambled aboard. Ponce suffered pains from his soon-to-be-fatal wound, and Juarez lay in the sand. The expedition leaders would never make it back to Spain.

The ship's sails unfurled, and she began to sail away. Petnima took ten steps away from Gurefin and Targonsa. She hadn't seen how Juarez had come to be laid out in the sand. Gurefin and Targonsa began to laugh.

"Stop laughing. It's not funny. He was a good man." She closed her eyes and sobbed.

"He must have had enough of the pure water—look."

Petnima opened her eyes and watched Juarez pick himself up out of the surf, holding the arrow he had stuck in the sand next to him.

ABOUT THE AUTHOR

Author Jim Halverson grew up in the rural gold-mining town of Mokelumne Hill, California, and received his MBA from Golden Gate University. He spent part of his life on a ranch and is an avid student of psychology. He recognizes the struggles of all people seeking equality and respect.

Jim and his wife, Gail, spend their free time traveling from their small farm in Forestville, California, to high-desert parts of the west, and wild untamed lands around the world.

Long ago, Jim received an essay back from his professor with a cryptic note: "Why don't you write about something you know?" The result was a paper the professor shared with the rest of the English department. That lesson was not wasted. For more information visit www.jhalverson.com.